WAITING *for an* ANGEL

WAITING *for an* ANGEL

HELON HABILA

W. W. NORTON & COMPANY   NEW YORK   LONDON

Manufacturing by The Haddon Craftsmen, Inc.
Book design by Chris Welch
Production manager: Amanda Morrison

Library of Congress Cataloging-in-Publication Data
Habila, Helon.
Waiting for an angel / Helon Habila.— 1st American ed.
p. cm.
ISBN 0-393-05193-5
1. Political prisoners—Fiction. 2. Nigeria—Fiction.
I. Title.
PR9387.9.H26 W34 2003
823'.92—dc21   2002026595

W. W. Norton & Company, Inc., 500 Fifth Avenue,
New York, N.Y. 10110
www.wwnorton.com

W. W. Norton & Company Ltd., Castle House,
75/76 Wells Street, London W1T 3QT

1 2 3 4 5 6 7 8 9 0

DEDICATION

For my family
My mother, Alheri Habila,
My sisters, Ruth and Briskilla,
My brothers, Dauda, Sulaiman, Ezra, Obed, Filibus, Bitrus
and Andrew,
And the memory of my father, Habila Ngalabak.
And for Sue.

PUBLISHER'S NOTE

Parts of this book first appeared in somewhat different form in *Prison Stories*, first published in 2000 by Epik Books in Lagos. The opening section, 'Lomba' (previously titled 'Love Poems'), won the Caine Prize for African Writing in 2001.

CONTENTS

ACKNOWLEDGEMENTS

I wish to thank certain people for their support in the course of bringing this book to reality. My cousin Bada, and his wife, Janet, and his mother-in-law, Ms Shatu Garba, thanks for your love and encouragement; Hannah Griffiths, thanks for being so indispensible; Simon Prosser, thanks for your invaluable suggestions and patience. I must also thank Nick and Helen Elam, Dan Jacobson, Baroness Nicholson, Jonathan Taylor, and all of the Caine Prize people for taking such a special interest in my writing. Thank you all.

WAITING *for an* ANGEL

LOMBA

IN THE MIDDLE of his second year in prison, Lomba got
access to pencil and paper and he started a diary. It was not
easy. He had to write in secret, mostly in the early mornings
when the night warders, tired of peeping through the door
bars, waited impatiently for the morning shift. Most of the
entries he simply headed with the days of the week; the exact
dates, when he used them, were often incorrect. The first
entry was in July 1997, a Friday.

Friday, July 1997
Today I begin a diary, to say all the things I want to say, to
myself, because here in prison there is no one to listen. I

express myself. It stops me from standing in the centre of this narrow cell and screaming at the top of my voice. It stops me from jumping up suddenly and bashing my head repeatedly against the wall. Prison chains not so much your hands and feet as it does your voice.

I express myself. I let my mind soar above these walls to bring back distant, exotic bricks with which I seek to build a more endurable cell within this cell. Prison. Misprison. Dis. Un. Prisoner. See? I write of my state in words of derision, aiming thereby to reduce the weight of these walls on my shoulders, to rediscover my nullified individuality. Here in prison loss of self is often expressed as anger. Anger is the baffled prisoner's attempt to re-crystallize his slowly dissolving self. The anger creeps up on you, like twilight edging out the day. It builds in you silently until one day it explodes in violence, surprising you. I saw it happen in my first month in prison. A prisoner, without provocation, had attacked an unwary warder at the toilets. The prisoner had come out of a bath-stall and there was the warder before him, monitoring the morning ablutions. Suddenly the prisoner leaped upon him, pulling him by the neck to the ground, grinding him into the black, slimy water that ran in the gutter from the toilets. He pummelled the surprised face repeatedly until other warders came and dragged him away. They beat him to a pulp before throwing him into solitary.

SOMETIMES THE ANGER leaves you as suddenly as it appeared; then you enter a state of tranquil acceptance. You

realize the absolute puerility of your anger: it was nothing
but acid, cancer, eating away your bowels in the dark. You
accept the inescapability of your fate; and with that, you
learn the craft of cunning. You learn ways of surviving —
surviving the mindless banality of the walls around you, the
incessant harassment from the warders; you learn to hide
money in your anus, to hold a cigarette inside your mouth
without wetting it. And each day survived is a victory against
the jailer, a blow struck for freedom.

My anger lasted a whole year. I remember the exact day it
left me. It was a Saturday, the day after a failed escape
attempt by two convicted murderers. The warders were
more than usually brutal that day; the inmates were on ten-
terhooks, not knowing from where the next blow would
come. We were lined up in rows in our cell, waiting for
hours to be addressed by the prison superintendent. When
he came his scowl was hard as rock, his eyes were red and
singeing, like fire. He paced up and down before us, systematically flagellating us with his harsh, staccato sentences.
We listened, our heads bowed, our hearts quaking.

When he left, an inmate, just back from a week in solitary, broke down and began to weep. His hands shook, as if
with a life of their own. 'What's going to happen next?' he
wailed, going from person to person, looking into each face,
not waiting for an answer. 'We'll be punished. If I go back
there I'll die. I can't. I can't.' Now he was standing before
me, a skinny mass of eczema inflammations, and ringworm,
and snot. He couldn't be more than twenty, I thought; what
did he do to end up in this dungeon? Then, without think-

ing, I reached out and patted his shoulder. I even smiled. With a confidence I did not feel I said kindly, 'No one will take you back.' He collapsed into my arms, soaking my shirt with snot and tears and saliva. 'Everything will be all right,' I repeated over and over. That was the day the anger left me.

IN THE OVER two months that he wrote before he was discovered and his diary seized, Lomba managed to put in quite a large number of entries. Most of them were poems, and letters to various persons from his by now hazy, pre-prison life — letters he can't have meant to send. There were also long soliloquies and desultory interior monologues. The poems were mostly love poems; fugitive lines from poets he had read in school: Donne, Shakespeare, Graves, Eliot, etc. Some were his original compositions rewritten from memory; but a lot were fresh creations — tortured sentimental effusions to women he had known and admired, and perhaps loved. Of course they might have been imaginary beings, fabricated in the smithy of his prison-fevered mind. One of the poems reads like a prayer to a much doubted, but fervently hoped for God:

Lord, I've had days black as pitch
And nights crimson as blood,

But they have passed over me, like water.
Let this one also pass over me, lightly,
Like a smooth rock rolling down the hill,
Down my back, my skin, like soothing water.

That, he wrote, was the prayer on his lips the day the cell door opened without warning and the superintendent, flanked by two baton-carrying warders, entered.

Monday, September
I had waited for this; perversely anticipated it with each day that passed, with each surreptitious sentence that I wrote. I knew it was me he came for when he stood there, looking bigger than life, bigger than the low, narrow cell. The two dogs with him licked their chops and growled. Their eyes roved hungrily over the petrified inmates caught sitting, or standing, or crouching; laughing, frowning, scratching — like figures in a movie still.

'Lomba, step forward!' his voice rang out suddenly. In the frozen silence it sounded like glass breaking on concrete, but harsher, without the tinkling. I was on my mattress on the floor, my back propped against the damp wall. I stood up. I stepped forward.

He turned the scowl on me. 'So, Lomba. You are.'

'Yes. I am Lomba,' I said. My voice did not fail me. Then he nodded, almost imperceptibly, to the two warders. They bounded forward eagerly, like game hounds scenting a rabbit. One went to a tiny crevice low in the wall, almost hidden by my mattress. He threw aside the mattress and poked two fingers into the triangular crack. He came out with a thick roll of papers. He looked triumphant as he handed it to the superintendent. Their informer had been exact. The other hound reached unerringly into a tiny hole in the sagging, rain-patterned ceiling and brought out another tube of papers.

'Search. More!' the superintendent barked. He unrolled the tubes. He appeared surprised at the number of sheets in his hands. I was. I didn't know I had written so much. When they were through with the holes and crevices, the dogs turned their noses to my personal effects. They picked up my mattress and shook and sniffed and poked. They ripped off the tattered cloth on its back. There were no papers there. They took the pillow-cum-rucksack (a jeans trouser-leg cut off at mid-thigh and knotted at the ankle) and poured out the contents on to the floor. Two threadbare shirts, one pair of trousers, one plastic comb, one toothbrush, one half-used bar of soap, and a pencil. This is the sum of my life, I thought. This is what I've finally shrunk to; the detritus after the explosion: a comb, a toothbrush, soap, two shirts, one pair of trousers and a pencil. They swooped on the pencil before it had finished rolling on the floor, almost knocking heads in their haste.

'A pencil!' the superintendent said, shaking his head, exaggerating his amazement. The prisoners were standing in a tight, silent arc. He walked the length of the arc, displaying the papers and pencil, clucking his tongue. 'Papers. And pencil. In prison. Can you believe that? In my prison!'

I was sandwiched between the two hounds, watching the drama in silence. I felt removed from it all. Now the superintendent finally turned to me. He bent a little at the waist, pushing his face into mine. I smelt his grating smell; I picked out the white roots beneath his carefully dyed moustache.

'I will ask. Once. Who gave you. Papers?' He spoke like that, in jerky, truncated sentences.

I shook my head. I did my best to meet his red-hot glare. 'I don't know.'

Some of the inmates gasped, shocked; they mistook my answer for reckless intrepidity. They thought I was foolishly trying to protect my source. But in a few other eyes I saw sympathy. They understood that I had really forgotten where the papers came from.

'Hmm,' the superintendent growled. His eyes were on the papers in his hands; he kept folding and unfolding them. I was surprised he had not pounced on me yet. Maybe he was giving me a spell to reconsider my hopeless decision to protect whoever it was I was protecting. The papers. They might have blown in through the door bars on the sentinel wind that sometimes patrolled the prison yard in the evenings. Maybe a sympathetic warder, seeing my yearning for self-expression emblazoned neon-like on my face, had secretly thrust the roll of papers into my hands as he passed me in the yard. Maybe — and this seems more probable — I bought them from another inmate (anything can be bought here in prison, from marijuana to a gun). But I had forgotten. In prison, memory short-circuit is an ally to be cultivated at all costs.

'I repeat. My question. Who gave you the papers?' he thundered into my face, spraying me with spit.

I shook my head. 'I have forgotten.'

I did not see it, but he must have nodded to one of the hounds. All I felt was the crushing blow on the back of my neck. I pitched forward, stunned by pain and the unexpectedness of it. My face struck the door bars and I fell before the superintendent's boots. I saw blood where my face had touched the floor. I waited. I stared, mesmerized, at the reflection of my eyes in the high gloss of the boots' toecaps. One boot rose and landed on my neck, grinding my face into the floor.

'So. You won't. Talk. You think you are. Tough,' he shouted. 'You are. Wrong. Twenty years! That is how long I have been dealing with miserable bastards like you. Let this be an example to all of you. Don't. Think you can deceive me. We have our sources of information. You can't. This insect will be taken to solitary and he will be properly dealt with. Until. He is willing to. Talk.'

I imagined his eyes rolling balefully round the tight, narrow cell, branding each of the sixty inmates separately. The boot pressed down harder on my neck; I felt a tooth bend at the root.

'Don't think because you are political. Detainees you are untouchable. Wrong. You are all rats. Saboteurs. Anti-government rats. That is all. Rats.'

But the superintendent was too well versed in the ways of torture to throw me into solitary that very day. I waited two days before they came and blindfolded me and took me away to the solitary section. In the night. Forty-eight hours. In the first twenty-four hours I waited with my eyes fixed on the door, bracing myself whenever it opened; but it was only the cooks bringing the meal, or the number-check warders come to count the inmates for the night, or the slop-disposal team. In the second twenty-four hours I bowed my head into my chest and refused to look up. I was tired. I refused to eat or speak or move. I was rehearsing for solitary.

———

THEY CAME, AT around ten at night. The two hounds. Banging their batons on the door bars, shouting my name, cursing and kicking at anyone in their path. I hastened to my feet before they reached me, my trouser-leg rucksack clutched like a shield in my hands. The light of their torch on my face was like a blow.

'Lomba!'

'Come here! Move!'

'Oya, out. Now!'

I moved, stepping high over the stirring bodies on the floor. The light fell on my rucksack.

'What's that in your hand, eh? Where you think say you dey carry am go? Bring am. Come here! Move!'

OUTSIDE. THE CELL door clanked shut behind us. All the compounds were in darkness. Only security lights from poles shone at the sentry posts. In the distance, the prison wall loomed huge and merciless, like a mountain. Broken bottles. Barbed wire. Then they threw the blindfold over my head. My hands instinctively started to rise, but they were held and forced behind me and cuffed.

'Follow me.'

One was before me, the other was behind, prodding me with his baton. I followed the footsteps, stumbling. At first it was easy to say where we were. There were eight compounds within the prison yard; ours was the only one reserved for political detainees. There were four other Awaiting Trial men's compounds surrounding ours. Of the three compounds for convicted criminals, one was for lifers and one, situated far away from the other compounds, was for condemned criminals. Now we had passed the central lawn where the warders conducted their morning parade. We turned left towards the convicted prisoners' compounds, then right towards . . . we turned right again, then straight . . . I followed the boots, now totally disoriented. I realized that the forced march had no purpose to it, or rather its purpose was not to reach anywhere immediately. It was part of the torture. I walked. On and on. I bumped into the front warder whenever he stopped abruptly.

'What? You no de see? Idiot!'

Sometimes I heard their voices exchanging pleasantries and amused chuckles with other warders. We marched for over thirty minutes; my slippered feet were chipped and bloody from hitting into stones. My arms locked behind me robbed me of balance and often I fell down, then I'd be prodded and kicked. At some places — near the light poles — I was able to see brief shimmers of light. At other places the darkness was thick as walls, and eerie. I recalled the shuffling, chain-clanging steps we heard late at nights through our cell window. Reluctant, sad steps. Hanging victims going to the hanging room; or their ghosts returning. We'd lie in the dark, stricken by immobility as the shuffling grew distant and finally faded away.

Now we were on concrete, like a corridor. The steps in front halted. I waited. I heard metal knock against metal, then the creaking of hinges. A hand took my wrist, cold metal touched me as the handcuffs were unlocked. My hands felt light with relief. I must have been standing right before the cell door because when a hand on my back pushed me forward I stumbled inside. I was still blindfolded, but I felt the consistency of the darkness change: it grew thicker, I had to wade through it to feel the walls. That was all: walls so close together that I felt like a man in a hole. I reached down and touched a bunk. I sat down. I heard the door close. I heard footsteps retreating. When I removed the blindfold the darkness remained the same, only now a little air touched my face. I closed my eyes. I don't know how long I remained like that, hunched forward on the bunk, my sore, throbbing feet on the floor, my elbows on my knees, my eyes closed.

As if realizing how close I was to tears, the smells got up from their corners, shook the dust off their buttocks and lined up to make my acquaintance — to distract me from my sad thoughts. I shook their hands one by one: Loneliness Smell, Anger Smell, Waiting Smell, Masturbation Smell, Fear Smell. The most noticeable was Fear Smell; it filled the tiny room from floor to ceiling, edging out the others. I did not cry. I opened my lips and slowly, like a Buddhist chanting his mantra, I prayed:

Let this one also pass over me, lightly,
Like a smooth rock rolling down the hill,
Down my back, my skin, like soothing water.

HE WAS IN solitary for three days. This is how he described the cell in his diary: *The floor was about six feet by ten, and the ceiling was about seven feet from the floor. There were two*

*pieces of furniture: the iron bunk with its tattered, lice-ridden
mat, and the slop bucket in the corner.*

His only contact with the outside was when his mess of
beans, once daily at six p.m., was pushed into the cell
through a tiny flap at the bottom of the wrought-iron door,
and at precisely eight p.m. when the cell door was opened for
him to take out the slop bucket and replace it with a fresh
one. He wrote that the only way he distinguished night from
day was by the movement of his bowels — in hunger or in
purgation.

Then on the third day, late in the evening, things began to
happen. Like Nichodemus, the superintendent came to him,
covertly, seeking knowledge.

Third Day. Solitary Cell

When I heard metal touch the lock on the door I sat down
from my blind pacing. I composed my countenance. The
door opened, bringing in unaccustomed rays of light. I
blinked. *'Oh, sweet light, may your face meeting mine bring
me good fortune.'* When my eyes had adjusted to the light,
the superintendent was standing on the threshold — the
cell entrance was a tight, brightly lit frame around his loom-
ing form. He advanced into the cell and stood in the centre,
before me in my disadvantaged position on the bunk. His
legs were planted apart, like an A. He looked like a cartoon
figure: his jodhpur-like uniform trousers emphasized the
skinniness of his calves, where they disappeared into the
glass-glossy boots. His stomach bulged and hung like a
belted sack. He cleared his voice. When I looked at his face

I saw his blubber lips twitching with the effort of an attempted smile. But he couldn't quite carry it off. He started to speak, then stopped abruptly and began to pace the tiny space before the bunk. When he returned to his original position he stopped. Now I noticed the sheaf of papers in his hands. He gestured in my face with it.

'These. Are the. Your papers.' His English was more disfigured than usual. He was soaking wet with the effort of saying whatever it was he wanted to say. 'I read. All. I read your file again. Also. You are journalist. This is your second year. Here. Awaiting trial. For organizing violence. Demonstration against. Anti-government demonstration against the military legal government.' He did not thunder as usual.

'It is not true.'

'Eh?' The surprise on his face was comical. 'You deny?'

'I did not organize a demonstration. I went there as a reporter.'

'Well . . .' He shrugged. 'That is not my business. The truth. Will come out at your. Trial.'

'But when will that be? I have been forgotten. I am not allowed a lawyer, or visitors. I have been awaiting trial for two years now . . .'

'Do you complain? Look. Twenty years I've worked in prisons all over this country. Nigeria. North. South. East. West. Twenty years. Don't be stupid. Sometimes it is better this way. How. Can you win a case against government? Wait. Hope.'

Now he lowered his voice, like a conspirator. 'Maybe there'll be another coup, eh? Maybe the leader will collapse and die. He is mortal, after all. Maybe a civilian government will come. Then. There will be amnesty for all political prisoners. Amnesty. Don't worry. Enjoy yourself.'

I looked at him, planted before me like a tree, his hands clasped behind him, the papier-mâché smile on his lips. *Enjoy yourself.* I turned the phrase over and over in my mind. When I lay to sleep rats kept me awake, and mosquitoes, and lice, and hunger, and loneliness. The rats bit at my toes and scuttled around in the low ceiling, sometimes falling on to my face from the holes in the ceiling. *Enjoy yourself.*

'Your papers,' he said, thrusting them at me once more. I was not sure if he was offering them to me. 'I read them. All. Poems. Letters. Poems, no problem. The letters, illegal. I burned them. Prisoners sometimes smuggle out letters to the press to make us look foolish. Embarrass the government. But the poems are harmless. Love poems. And diaries. You wrote the poems for your girl, isn't it?'

He bent forward, and clapped a hand on my shoulder. I realized with wonder that the man, in his awkward, flat-footed way, was making overtures of friendship to me. My eyes fell on the boot that had stepped on my neck just five days ago. What did he want?

'Perhaps because I work in prison. I wear uniform. You think I don't know poetry, eh? Soyinka, Okigbo, Shakespeare.'

It was apparent that he wanted to talk about poems, but he was finding it hard to begin.

'What do you want?' I asked.

He drew back to his full height. 'I write poems too. Sometimes,' he added quickly when the wonder grew and grew on my face. He dipped his hand into his jacket pocket and came out with a foolscap sheet of paper. He unfolded it and handed it to me. 'Read.'

It was a poem; handwritten. The title was written in capital letters: 'MY LOVE FOR YOU'.

Like a man in a dream, I ran my eyes over the bold squiggles. After the first stanza I saw that it was a thinly veiled imitation of one of my poems. I sensed his waiting. He was hardly breathing. I let him wait. Lord, I can't remember another time when I had felt so good. So powerful. I was Samuel Johnson and he was an aspiring poet waiting anxiously for my verdict, asking tremulously, 'Sir, is it poetry, is it Pindar?'

I wanted to say, with as much sarcasm as I could put into my voice, 'Sir, your poem is both original and interesting, but the part that is interesting is not original, and the part that is original is not interesting.' But all I said was, 'Not bad, you need to work on it some more.'

The eagerness went out of his face and for a fleeting moment the scowl returned. 'I promised my lady a poem. She is educated, you know. A teacher. You will write a poem for me. For my lady.'

'You want me to write a poem for you?' I tried to mask the surprise, the confusion and, yes, the eagerness in my voice. He was offering me a chance to write.

'I am glad you understand. Her name is Janice. She has been to the university. She has class. Not like other girls. She teaches in my son's school. That is how we met.'

Even jailers fall in love, I thought inanely.

'At first she didn't take me seriously. She thought I only wanted to use her and dump her. And. Also. We are of differ-

ent religion. She is Christian, I am Muslim. But no problem.
I love her. But she still doubted. I did not know what to do.
Then I saw one of your poems . . . yes, this one.' He handed
me the poem. 'It said everything I wanted to tell her.'

It was one of my early poems, rewritten from memory.

'"Three Words". I gave it to her yesterday when I took her
out.'

'You gave her my poem?'

'Yes.'

'You . . . you told her you wrote it?'

'Yes, yes, of course. I wrote it again in my own hand,' he
said, unabashed. He had been speaking in a rush; now he
drew himself together and, as though to reassert his authority, began to pace the room, speaking in a subdued, mea-
sured tone. 'I can make life easy for you here. I am the
prison superintendent. There is nothing I cannot do, if I
want. So write. The poem. For me.'

There is nothing I cannot do. You can get me cigarettes, I
am sure, and food. You can remove me from solitary. But can
you stand me outside these walls, free under the stars? Can
you connect the tips of my upraised arms to the stars so that
the surge of liberty passes down my body to the soft downy
grass beneath my feet?

I asked for paper and pencil. And a book to read.

HE WAS REMOVED from the solitary section that day. The
pencil and paper came, the book too. But not the one he had
asked for. He wanted Wole Soyinka's prison notes, *The Man*

Died; but when it came it was *A Brief History of West Africa*. While writing the poems in the cell, Lomba would sometimes let his mind wander; he'd picture the superintendent and his lady out on a date, how he'd bring out the poem and unfold it and hand it to her and say boldly, 'I wrote it for you. Myself.'

THEY SIT OUTSIDE on the verandah at her suggestion. The light from the hanging, wind-swayed Chinese lanterns falls softly on them. The breeze blowing from the lagoon below smells fresh to her nostrils; she loves its dampness on her bare arms and face. She looks at him across the circular table, with its vase holding a single rose. He appears nervous. A thin film of sweat covers his forehead. He removes his cap and dabs at his forehead with a white handkerchief.

'Do you like it, a Chinese restaurant?' he asks, like a father anxious to please his favourite child. It is their first outing together. He pestered her until she gave in. Sometimes she is at a loss what to make of his attentions. She sighs. She turns her plump face to the deep, blue lagoon. A white boat with dark stripes on its sides speeds past; a figure is crouched inside, almost invisible. Her light, flower-patterned gown shivers in the light breeze. She watches him covertly. He handles his chopsticks awkwardly, but determinedly.

'Waiter!' he barks, his mouth full of fish, startling her. 'Bring another bottle of wine!'

'No. I am all right, really,' she says firmly, putting down her chopsticks.

———

AFTER THE MEAL, which has been quite delicious, he lifts the tiny, wine-filled porcelain cup before him and says: 'To you. And me.'

She sips her drink, avoiding his eyes.

'I love you, Janice. Very much. I know you think I am not serious. That I only want to suck. The juice and throw away the peel. No.' He suddenly dips his hand into the pocket of his well-ironed white kaftan and brings out a yellow paper.

'Read and see.' He pushes the paper across the table to her. 'I wrote it. For you. A poem.'

She opens the paper. It smells faintly of sandalwood. She looks at the title: 'Three Words'. She reaches past the vase with its single, white rose, past the wine bottle, the wine glasses, and covers his hairy hand with hers briefly. 'Thank you.'

She reads the poem, shifting in her seat towards the swaying light of the lantern:

Three words

When I hear the waterfall clarity of your laughter,
When I see the twilight softness of your eyes,

I feel like draping you all over myself, like a cloak,
To be warmed by your warmth.

Your flower-petal innocence, your perennial
Sapling resilience — your endless charms

All these set my mind on wild flights of fancy:
I add word unto word,
I compare adjectives and coin exotic phrases

But they all seem jaded, corny, unworthy
Of saying all I want to say to you.

So I take refuge in these simple words,
Trusting my tone, my hand in yours, when I
Whisper them, to add depth and new
Twists of meaning to them. Three words:
I love you.

WITH HIS THIRD or fourth poem for the superintendent, Lomba began to send Janice cryptic messages. She seemed to possess an insatiable appetite for love poems. Every day a warder came to the cell, in the evening, with the same request from the superintendent: 'The poem.' When he finally ran out of original poems, Lomba began to plagiarize the masters from memory. Here are the opening lines of one:

Janice, your beauty is to me
Like those treasures of gold . . .

Another one starts:

I wonder, my heart, what you and I
Did till we loved . . .

But it was Lomba's bowdlerization of Sappho's 'Ode' that brought the superintendent to the cell door:

A peer of goddesses she seems to me
The lady who sits over against me
Face to face,

Listening to the sweet tones of my voice,
And the loveliness of my laughing.
It is this that sets my heart fluttering
In my chest,
For if I gaze on you but for a little while
I am no longer master of my voice,
And my tongue lies useless
And a delicate flame runs over my skin
No more do I see with my eyes;
The sweat pours down me
I am all seized with trembling
And I grow paler than the grass
My strength fails me
And I seem little short of dying.

HE CAME TO the cell door less than twenty minutes after the poem had reached him, waving the paper in the air, a real smile splitting his granite face.

'Lomba, come out!' he hollered through the iron bars. Lomba was lying on his wafer-thin mattress, on his back, trying to imagine figures out of the rain designs on the ceiling. The door officer hastily threw open the door.

The superintendent threw a friendly arm over Lomba's shoulders. He was unable to stand still. He walked Lomba up and down the grassy courtyard.

'This poem. Excellent. With this poem. After. I'll ask her for marriage.' He was incoherent in his excitement. He raised the paper and read aloud the first line, straining his eyes in the dying light: '"A peer of goddesses she seems to me". Yes.

Excellent. She will be happy. Do you think I should ask her for. Marriage. Today?'

He stood before Lomba, bent forward expectantly, his legs planted in their characteristic A formation.

'Why not?' Lomba answered. A passing warder stared at the superintendent and the prisoner curiously. Twilight fell dully on the broken bottles studded in the concrete of the prison wall.

'Yes. Why not. Good.' The superintendent walked up and down, his hands clasped behind him, his head bowed in thought. Finally, he stopped before Lomba and declared gravely: 'Tonight. I'll ask her.'

Lomba smiled at him, sadly. The superintendent saw the smile; he did not see the sadness.

'Good. You are happy. I am happy too. I'll send you a packet of cigarettes. Two packets. Today. Enjoy. Now go back inside.'

He turned abruptly on his heels and marched away.

September

Janice came to see me two days after I wrote her the Sappho. I thought, she has discovered my secret messages, my scriptive Morse tucked innocently in the lines of the poems I've written her.

Two o'clock is compulsory siesta time. The opening of the cell door brought me awake. My limbs felt heavy and lifeless. I feared I might have an infection. The warder came directly to me.

'Oya, get up. The superintendent wan see you.' His skin was coarse, coal black. He was fat and his speech came out in laboured gasps. 'Oya, get up. Get up,' he repeated impatiently.

I was in that lethargic, somnambulistic state condemned people surely fall into when, in total inanition and despair, they await their fate — without fear or hope, because nothing can be changed. No dew-wet finger of light would come poking into the parched gloom of the abyss they tenant. I did not want to write any more poems for the superintendent's lover. I did not want any more of his cigarettes. I was tired of being pointed at behind my back, of being whispered about by the other inmates as the superintendent's informer, his fetch-water. I wanted to recover my lost dignity. Now I realized that I really had no 'self' to express; that self had flown away from me the day the chains touched my hands. What is left here is nothing but a mass of protruding bones, unkempt hair and tearful eyes; an asshole for shitting and farting, and a penis that in the mornings grows turgid in vain. This leftover self, this sea-bleached wreck panting on the iron-filing sands of the shores of this penal island is nothing but hot air, and hair, and ears cocked, hopeful . . .

So I said to the warder, 'I don't want to see him today. Tell him I'm sick.'

The fat face contorted. He raised his baton in Pavlovian response. 'What!' But our eyes met. He was smart enough to decipher the bold 'No Trespassing' sign written in mine. Smart enough to obey. He moved back, shrugging. 'Na you go suffer!' he blustered, and left.

I was aware of the curious eyes staring at me. I closed mine. I willed my mind over the prison walls to other places. Free. I dreamt of standing under the stars, my hands raised, their tips touching the blinking, pulsating electricity of the stars. The rain would be falling. There'd be nothing else: just me and rain and stars and my feet on the wet, downy grass earthing the electricity of freedom.

He returned almost immediately. There was a smirk on his fat face as he handed me a note. I recognized the superintendent's clumsy scrawl. It was brief, a one-liner: *Janice is here. Come. Now.* Truncated, even in writing. I got up and pulled on my sweat-grimed shirt. I slipped my feet into my old, worn-out slippers. I followed the warder. We passed the parade ground, and the convicted men's compound. An iron gate, far to our right, locked permanently, led to the women's wing of the prison. We passed the old laundry, which now served as a barber's shop on Saturdays — the prison's sanitation day. A gun-carrying warder opened a tiny door in the huge gate that led into a foreyard where the prison officials had their offices. I had been here before, once, on my first day in prison. There were cars parked before the offices; cadets in their well-starched uniforms came and went, their young faces looking comically stern. Female secretaries with time on their hands stood in the corridors gossiping. The superintendent's office was not far from the gate; a flight of three concrete steps led up to a thick wooden door, which bore the single word: SUPERINTENDENT.

My guide knocked on it timidly before turning the handle.

'The superintendent wan see am,' he informed the secretary. She barely looked up from her typewriter; she nodded. Her eyes were bored, uncurious.

'Enter,' the warder said to me, pointing to a curtained doorway beside the secretary's table. I entered. A lady sat in one of the two visitors' armchairs. Back to the door, her elbows rested on the huge Formica-topped table before her.

Janice. She was alone. When she turned, I noted that my mental image of her was almost accurate. She was plump. Her face was warm and homely. She came halfway out of her chair, turning it slightly so that it faced the other chair. There was a tentative smile on her face as she asked, 'Mr Lomba?'

I almost said no, surprised by the 'Mr'. I nodded.

She pointed at the empty chair. 'Please sit down.' She extended a soft, pudgy hand to me. I took it and marvelled at its softness. She was a teacher; the hardness would be in the fingers: the tips of the thumb and the middle finger, and the side of the index finger.

'Muftau — the superintendent — will be here soon. He just stepped out,' she said. Her voice was clear, a little high-pitched. Her English was correct, each word carefully pronounced and projected. Like in a classroom. I was struck by how clean she looked, squeaky clean; her skin glowed like a child's after a bath. She had obviously taken a lot of trouble with her appearance: her blue evening dress looked almost new, but a slash of red lipstick extended to the left cheek after missing the curve of the lip. She crossed and uncrossed her legs, tapping the left foot on the floor. She was nervous. That was when I realized I had not said a word since I entered.

'Welcome to the prison,' I said, unable to think of anything else.

She nodded. 'Thank you. I told Muftau I wanted to see you. The poems, I just knew it wasn't him writing them. I went along with it for a while, but later I told him.'

She opened the tiny handbag in her lap and took out

some papers. The poems. She put them on the table and unfolded them, smoothing out the creases, uncurling the edges. 'After the Sappho I decided I must see you. It was my favourite poem in school, and I like your version of it.'

'Thank you,' I said. I liked her directness, her sense of humour.

'So I told him — look, I know who the writer is, he is one of the prisoners, isn't he? That surprised him. He couldn't figure out how I knew. But I was glad he didn't deny it. I told him that. And if we are getting married, there shouldn't be secrets between us, should there?'

Ah, I thought, so my Sappho has worked the magic. Aloud I said, 'Congratulations.'

She nodded. 'Thanks. Muftau is a nice person, really, when you get to know him. His son, Farouk, was in my class — he's finished now — really, you should see them together. So touching. I know he has his awkward side, and that he was once married — but I don't care. After all, I have a little past too. Who doesn't?' She added the last quickly, as if scared she was revealing too much to a stranger. Her left hand went up and down as she spoke, like a hypnotist, like a conductor. After a brief pause, she continued, 'After all the pain he's been through with his other wife, he deserves some happiness. She was in the hospital a whole year before she died.'

Muftau. The superintendent had a name, and a history, maybe even a soul. I looked at his portrait hanging on the wall. He looked young in it, serious-faced and smart, like the cadet warders outside. I turned to her and said suddenly and sincerely, 'I am glad you came. Thanks.'

Her face broke into a wide, dimpled smile. She was actually pretty. A little past her prime, past her sell-by date, but still nice, still viable. 'Oh, no. I am the one that should be glad. I love meeting poets. I love your poems. Really I do.'

'Not all of them are mine.'

'I know — but you give them a different feel, a different tone. And also, I discovered your S.O.S. I had to come . . .' She picked the poems off the table and handed them to me. There were thirteen of them. Seven were my originals, six were purloined. She had carefully underlined in red ink certain lines in some of them — the same line, actually, recurring.

There was a waiting-to-be-congratulated smile on her face as she awaited my comment.

'You noticed,' I said.

'Of course I did. S.O.S. It wasn't apparent at first. I began to notice the repetition with the fifth poem. "Save my soul, a prisoner."'

'Save my soul, a prisoner' . . . The first time I put down the words, in the third poem, it had been non-deliberate, I was just making alliteration. Then I began to repeat it in the subsequent poems. But how could I tell her that the message wasn't really for her, or for anyone else? It was for myself, perhaps, written by me to my own soul, to every other soul, the collective soul of the universe.

I told her, the first time I wrote it an inmate had died. His name was Thomas. He wasn't sick. He just started vomiting after the afternoon meal, and before the warders came to take him to the clinic, he died. Just like that. He died. Watching his stiffening face, with the mouth open and the eyes staring, as the inmates took him out of the cell, an irrational fear had gripped me. I saw myself being taken out like that, my lifeless arms dangling, brushing the ground. The fear made me sit down, shaking uncontrollably amidst the flurry of movements and voices excited by the tragedy. I was scared. I felt certain I was going to end up like that. Have you ever felt like that, certain that you are going to die? No? I did. I was going to die. My body would end up in some anonymous mortuary, and later in an unmarked grave, and no one would know. No one would care. It happens every day here. I am a political detainee; if I die I am just one antagonist less. That was when I wrote the S.O.S. It was just a message in a bottle, thrown without much hope into the sea . . . I stopped speaking when my hands started to shake. I wanted to put them in my pocket to hide them from her. But she had seen it. She left her seat and came to me. She took both my hands in hers.

'You'll not die. You'll get out alive. One day it will all be over,' she said. Her perfume, mixed with her female smell, rose into my nostrils: flowery, musky. I had forgotten the last time a woman had stood so close to me. Sometimes, in our cell, when the wind blows from the female prison, we'll catch distant sounds of female screams and shouts and even laughter. That is the closest we ever come to women. Only when the wind blows, at the right time, in the right direction. Her hands on mine, her smell, her presence, acted like fire on some huge, prehistoric glacier locked deep in my chest. And when her hand touched my head and the back of my neck, I wept.

When the superintendent returned, my sobbing face was buried in Janice's ample bosom. Her hands were on my head, patting, consoling, like a mother, all the while cooing softly, 'One day it will finish.'

I pulled away from her. She gave me her handkerchief.

'What is going on? Why is he crying?'

He was standing just within the door — his voice was curious, with a hint of jealousy. I wiped my eyes; I subdued my body's spasms. He advanced slowly into the room and went round to his seat. He remained standing, his hairy hands resting on the table.

'Why is he crying?' he repeated to Janice.

'Because he is a prisoner,' Janice replied simply. She was still standing beside me, facing the superintendent.

'Well. So? Is he realizing that just now?'

'Don't be so unkind, Muftau.'

I returned the handkerchief to her.

'Muftau, you must help him.'

'Help. How?'

'You are the prison superintendent. There's a lot you can do.'

'But I can't help him. He is a political detainee. He has not even been tried.'

'And you know that he is never going to be tried. He will be kept here for ever, forgotten.' Her voice became sharp and indignant. The superintendent drew back his seat and sat down. His eyes were lowered. When he looked up, he said earnestly, 'Janice. There's nothing anyone can do for him. I'll be implicating myself. Besides, his lot is far easier than that of other inmates. I give him things. Cigarettes. Soap. Books. And I let him. Write.'

'How can you be so unfeeling! Put yourself in his shoes

— two years away from friends, from family, without the power to do anything you wish to do. Two years in CHAINS! How can you talk of cigarettes and soap, as if that were substitute enough for all that he has lost?' She was like a teacher confronting an erring student. Her left hand tapped the table for emphasis as she spoke.

'Well.' He looked cowed. His scowl alternated rapidly with a smile. He stared at his portrait on the wall behind her. He spoke in a rush. 'Well. I could have done something. Two weeks ago. The Amnesty International. People came. You know, white men. They wanted names of. Political detainees held. Without trial. To pressure the government to release them.'

'Well?'

'Well.' He still avoided her stare. His eyes touched mine and hastily passed. He picked up a pen and twirled it between his fingers. The pen slipped out of his fingers and fell to the floor.

'I didn't. Couldn't. You know . . . I thought he was comfortable. And, he was writing the poems, for you . . .' His voice was almost pleading. Surprisingly, I felt no anger towards him. He was just Man. Man in his basic, rudimentary state, easily moved by powerful emotions like love, lust, anger, greed and fear, but totally dumb to the finer, acquired emotions like pity, mercy, humour and justice.

Janice slowly picked up her bag from the table. There was enormous dignity to her movements. She clasped the bag under her left arm. Her words were slow, almost sad. 'I see now that I've made a mistake. You are not really the man I thought you were . . .'

'Janice.' He stood up and started coming round to her, but a gesture stopped him.

'No. Let me finish. I want you to contact these people. Give them his name. If you can't do that, then forget you ever knew me.'

Her hand brushed my arm as she passed me. He started after her, then stopped halfway across the room. We stared in silence at the curtained doorway, listening to the sound of her heels on the bare floor till it finally died away. He returned slowly to his seat and slumped into it. The wood creaked audibly in the quiet office.

'Go,' he said, not looking at me.

THE ABOVE IS the last entry in Lomba's diary. There's no record of how far the superintendent went to help him regain his freedom, but as he told Janice, there was very little to be done for a political detainee — especially since, about a week after that meeting, a coup was attempted against the military leader, General Sani Abacha, by some officers close to him. There was an immediate crackdown on all pro-democracy activists, and the prisons all over the country swelled with political detainees. A lot of those already in detention were transferred randomly to other prisons around the country, for security reasons. Lomba was among them. He was transferred to Agodi Prison in Ibadan. From there he was moved to the far north, to a small desert town called Gashuwa. There is no record of him after that.

A lot of these political prisoners died in detention,

although only the prominent ones made the headlines — people like Moshood Abiola and General Yar Adua.

But somehow it is hard to imagine that Lomba died. A lot seems to point to the contrary. His diary, his economical expressions, show a very sedulous character at work. A survivor. The years in prison must have taught him not to hope too much, not to despair too much — that for the prisoner, nothing kills as surely as too much hope or too much despair. He had learned to survive in tiny atoms, piecemeal, a day at a time. It is probable that in 1998, when the military dictator Abacha died, and his successor, General Abdulsalam Abubakar, dared to open the gates to democracy, and to liberty for the political detainees, Lomba was in the ranks of those released.

This might have been how it happened: Lomba was seated in a dingy cell in Gashuwa, his eyes closed, his mind soaring above the glass-studded prison walls, mingling with the stars and the rain in elemental union of freedom; then the door clanked open, and when he opened his eyes Liberty was standing over him, smiling kindly, extending an arm.

And Liberty said softly, 'Come. It is time to go.'

And they left, arm in arm.

THE ANGEL

TODAY IS THE last day of my life.

I knew it when I woke up in the morning and saw a crow croaking on my window ledge. I shivered and waved the pillow at it. I watched it fly away through the trees, croaking till it disappeared.

'When your time comes, you'll know,' a marabout once told me.

Now I know; even if I hadn't seen the black bird I would have known.

Death hangs around me like a mist, and now as I sit by the window in this bar, waiting for the Angel of Death, I feel as if anyone that looks at me can see it.

'Only a blessed few can see Israfael, the Angel of Death, when he comes for them. His face is the most terrible thing to behold,' the marabout said. His words echo in my mind as if he is standing before me, uttering them. But it was six months ago that we went to him, Bola, Lomba and I. We had gone, on Lomba's suggestion, to Badagry to see the slave port, but halfway through the tour we wandered off, depressed by the guide's mournful and vivid descriptions of how the chains and mouth locks had been used on the slaves.

'There is a fortune-teller somewhere on the beach. Let's go to him,' Lomba said. But when we found him he told us he was not a fortune-teller.

He had a crude shed made of bamboo and raffia high on the cliff, overlooking the sea. He was seated on a flat rock before the shed, a skinny Buddha, facing the water. He was naked but for a goatskin around his waist; his skin was wrinkled and scaly from sunburn. His head was clean-shaven; his eyes were hooded, dreamy.

'I am a poet. I listen to the waves for tales of other shores and of the deep. Listen. Sit down,' he told us in a voice bleached by sea water.

We sat. We listened. The waves rose high as walls and broke with alarming violence against the rocks. I closed my eyes. I felt lulled by the alternating roar and silence. He said: 'Life is like a wave motion, full of highs and lows. We sit on life's shores with our hands open, waiting to receive. But the water knows, more than we do, what we need and what we don't need. It takes away from us what we don't need, and drops it at another shore where it is needed. Sometimes it returns to us what it took away, refined and augmented with brine and other sea minerals. The sea, like death, is not an end but a beginning. Beneath it there is no bed, but another surface, another air.'

He stood up suddenly. 'You kids have put me in a good mood today. Follow me into the shed, I'll tell your fortunes, but one by one.'

Lomba entered first. There was a determined look on his face, like someone set on knowing the truth though it may turn out to be bitter. As I waited for my turn, I tried to decide what I wanted to know. Perhaps I should ask for special prayers for my coming exams. Lomba avoided my eyes when he came out; there was a bemused look on his face.

'What did he say?' I asked.

Lomba shrugged. 'Prison. That was all he saw ahead of me. Go in, try your luck, ask for good fortune, don't ask too closely.'

But when I entered and opened my mouth, what came out was: 'I want to know when I am going to die.' The marabout closed the Koran before him and pierced me with his stare. He was seated far inside the shed, on a goatskin. There was a calabash full of sea water to his right. I was kneeling before him, my back to the door and the roaring sea outside.

'Ask for something else. I could give you herbs to transport you and your girlfriend on a trip of a thousand delights. I could teach you a prayer that attracts wealth like moths to a fire. But death — why?'

I shrugged. 'I am curious, that is all. I want to be ready.'

'A wise man is always ready for death. Assume it will come tomorrow, or in the next minute.'

I stood up to go. 'Thanks,' I said, unable to hide my disappointment.

He raised a hand, stopping me. 'Sit down. Tell me, how old are you?'

'I am twenty-one.'

'Ah, sweet youth. Your life has just started.' He sounded wistful, almost sad. 'Youth. That is one thing the waves never return to us. Once lost, it is gone for ever.'

I sat and watched in silence as he poured a white powder into the calabash of sea water. He stared into it intently, as if it held the answer to the mysteries of life and death, which indeed it might, then he looked at me and said, 'You'll know when your time comes. You are lucky, not many people are given that privilege. You'll also see Israfael, the Angel of Death, when he comes for you.'

I HAVE BEEN seated here all day, looking out through the window, sipping Coke. I watch each face that enters — one of them might be an angel disguised as a mortal. They are said to do that when they come to earth so as not to scare people with their terrible countenance. The sky above is becoming overcast; soon it will rain. Perhaps I should go home; maybe this is not the place appointed.

Sudden loud shouts draw my eyes to the street.

'Ole!'

'Thief! Catch am o!'

A mob wielding cudgels and cutlasses is hot on the heels of a youth who desperately crosses to the other side of the road, narrowly missing the fender of a truck. The mob follows, growing bigger as it goes. The youth, looking over his shoulder as he runs, crashes into a light pole and falls senseless to the ground. Before he can regain a second wind the mob is on him. I watch the cudgels rise and fall, I hear his wailing, ululating scream finally turn into a whimper. They pour petrol on him and set him ablaze. I watch the fiery figure dancing and falling until it finally subsides onto the pavement as a black, faintly glowing, twitching mass.

The Angel of Death is in the neighbourhood, and soon it will be my turn. But not in such an ignoble fashion. I want to go in a way that, a hundred years from now, people will look back at with awe and say, 'His death had meaning.' Like those Christians in ancient Rome who submitted themselves to be eaten by lions in the arena without raising a murmur. I call that symbolic death. If only I had a way of choosing the manner of my own death, if only I could make it spectacular and momentous . . .

Outside, the clouds have descended lower in the sky. Lightning flashes every once in a while, like a tear in the dark fabric of the sky; people hurry to get off the street as huge pellets of rain begin to fall. The bar is filling up fast: people with nowhere to sit line up against the counter, staring at the flickering TV screen behind the barman. Then suddenly the screen goes blank; the announcer's image is replaced by spongy white particles.

'Change the station,' someone shouts.

The barman changes to another channel — he keeps turning the knob, but no image appears.

'Maybe they've no light,' someone says.

'All of them? Impossible.'

'Turn on the radio,' another person suggests.

There are so many faces in the bar, so many bodies pressed together — men and women and children; one of them, I am sure, is an angel. I look at their hands to see if I can detect the tell-tale ends of flight feathers retracted in disguise. There must be something in the eyes surely to suggest . . .

'It is a coup!' the barman shouts, raising his hand for silence. The words pass from mouth to mouth round the room. Everyone falls silent, pressing closer to the radio on the counter. Martial music wafts out of the box to hover on the air above the sweating faces. After the martial music, a parade-ground-voiced general makes a lengthy announcement in which only the words 'dusk-to-dawn curfew' make any visible impact on the room. Suddenly everyone is scurrying out of the bar into the light rain outside.

Soon the streets will be taken over by military tanks and jeeps. People will lock their doors and turn off their lights and peer fearfully through chinks in their windows at the rain-washed, post-*coup d'état* streets.

Now I am the only one left in the bar. There is still an hour before the curfew begins. I notice the barman staring at me as he flicks a rag aimlessly up and down the counter. He stares at the clock above the door, then out at the deserted street.

'I will wait for an hour,' I say to myself. Perhaps this is not the place appointed. But I felt so sure watching the thief doing his *danse macabre*.

The barman comes over. 'Oga, I want to close.' He avoids my eyes. He is elderly. He has a soup stain on his right sleeve.

'I am waiting for a friend. I gave him this address,' I reply.

'Maybe he won't come, because of the curfew,' the barman says.

But just then the door is kicked open. We turn and stare as two soldiers enter, dripping wet from the rain, guns slung over their shoulders. The barman leaves me and rushes over to them, bowing obsequiously. I feel a strange tingling all over my body, as if an electric shock has passed through me. I look at the soldiers, trying to determine which of them is here for me. One is short and fair, the other is tall and dark; but angels can assume any form they want. The barman hurries to the bar to bring them drinks. I keep staring at them, guessing.

'Hey!' the short one shouts at me, 'go home. There's a curfew on.'

'It is not six yet,' I reply, glancing at the clock. The soldiers look surprised at my bold response; they whisper together, then the short one stands up and swaggers to my table. His gun is unslung, the barrel points casually in my direction.

'Get out,' he says.

An ugly birthmark covers the left side of his face.

'I am waiting for someone, and it may be you,' I reply, but before I finish speaking he lunges forward and clears the Coke bottle and the glass off my table with the barrel of his rifle. The glass and bottle break as they hit the floor; the noise they make fills the hall. Thunder roars outside, the rain falls harder. He points the gun at me and moves back. Those Christians, did their hands shake like mine are shaking now, did their foreheads glisten with sweat and their hearts threaten to fail as the lions bounded towards them in the

Colosseum? Did the gladiators' voices quaver as they chanted their death-disdaining salute to the emperor: 'Hail Caesar, we who are about to die salute thee!'?

My movement is too fast for the soldier because he isn't expecting it. In one motion I shove the table at him; the edge catches him in the stomach, knocking the gun out of his hands. He falls down on the floor amidst the broken glasses. I make a desperate rush for the door, but before I reach it I hear a warning bark: 'Stop or I shoot!'

It is the other soldier.

But when I turn it is not a soldier standing there. It is an angel. It opens its enormous wings and closes them again in a clapping motion. The air from the wings lifts me up and carries me out through the door. I land with a splash on the wet street. I am bleeding from the chest. I feel life draining out of me — through the haze I make out a huge bird shape flying out of the bar and ascending with the sound of a thousand wings. Then it is gone.

BOLA

BOLA WOKE UP sweating and shivering. His voice, croaky and hoarse, woke me up.

'Lomba, Lomba.'

It was not yet seven. His bed was tousled, the sheets hung down to the floor, the pillow was also on the floor; it was as if a company of obstreperous kids had played in the bed. His eyes were bleary, edged with rheum. I kicked my legs out of the sheets and went to him.

'What?'

'I couldn't sleep.'

He looked agitated. His lips were parched. I touched his forehead. It was hot and slick with sweat.

'You've a temperature. Fever.'

'I had a terrible dream and I couldn't sleep.'

'What about?'

'Dead bodies. Fire . . .' He clutched the sheet, trying hard to stop himself shaking. His eyes darted to the open window, where the soft morning light streamed in, cutting itself into wide, vertical sheets on the steel bars. I gave him time to calm down. Bola always was excitable, and last night there had been too much excitement. That was his complaint — the excitement had persisted into his sleep, like a residual current, making his dreams hyperactive and phantom-filled.

'Go back to sleep, you need more rest.' I picked up my toothbrush and a cup of water and went out to the verandah. The students, who should have been abustle taking their baths and getting set for lectures, sat idly outside their rooms, by the roadsides, in groups, discussing the boycott of lectures.

Bola came out and stood beside me.

'The boycott is on,' I said, my feelings uncertain.

I didn't want to increase Bola's agitation by telling him of it, but I also had a strong presentiment of something dark and scary lurking in the shadows, inching its way on to the forestage of our lives.

It had started yesterday at the rally, when my ears suddenly went dead and I couldn't hear a word of what Sankara was saying. Yet I could make out every word he shouted as he jumped and gesticulated before the students: as if the words were coming in through the pores on my skin; or maybe I was reading his lips.

'. . . I say we are tired of being tired!'

'Yes! Tell them, Sanke!'

'Great Nigerian students!'

'G-R-E-A-T!'

'Remember what Soyinka wrote, "The man dies in him who stands silent in the face of tyranny." And according to Amilcar Cabral, "Every onlooker is either a coward or a traitor." That is why we are here today — we can't continue to be onlookers when a handful of gun-toting thugs are determined to push our beloved nation over the precipice . . .'

I was the only one in the crowd who was not jumping up and down and gesticulating and urging Sankara on. Not because I didn't agree with his words; I did, but I was not moved. I felt cold; I felt like an impostor, out of place, and my ears deaf. Bola, beside me, was throwing punches in the air and shouting. Before me was a group of girls screaming themselves hoarse, their wigs bobbing and sinking like boats in a storm as they jumped up and down. One staggered backward and stepped on my toes, all the while giggling. Suddenly I felt trapped among the hundreds of jumping, shouting and sweating bodies.

I quietly slipped out of the crowd and stood alone, surveying it from a distance. Sankara looked exaggeratedly huge on the upturned drum; he was dressed in combat jacket and trousers; his wispy goatee hung like a comb from his chin. The upraised, urging fists below him formed a plinth, supporting him. His strong voice carried easily to where I stood: 'We are tired of phantom transition programmes that are nothing but grand designs to embezzle our money!'

'Down with the Junta!'

In the room, I buried my head in a novel, trying to screen out Sankara's voice trickling in through the window amidst the static of shouts and chants. Much later, when I had almost drifted off to sleep, Bola entered, flushed with excitement, spouting revolutionary talk.

'*Aluta continua! Victoria acerta!*' he shouted as he came to a stop in the middle of the room, facing me. The light bulb threw his shadow under his legs, thick and dark, like a blotch of ink.

I sat up and picked my novel off the floor. 'How did it go?'

'According to Martin Luther King, "It is the duty of every citizen to oppose unjust authority . . ."'

I covered my ears, glaring at him. 'Please. Cut that out. Just tell me what was finally decided.'

But he went on stubbornly, scolding me for 'deserting the cause'.

'How could you walk away when the great student body was on the move?' He paced up and down, clenching his fist and gesticulating wildly with it. Imitating Sankara, I thought.

'Just tell me what the great student body has agreed on,' I said, my voice becoming testy.

'Can't you see what is happening? The military have turned the country into one huge barracks, into a prison. Every street out there is crawling with them; the people lock their doors, scared to come out. They play with us, as if we are puppets. Yesterday they changed the transition date again. IBB is deceiving us, he has no intention of leaving. It is our duty to push him out. We have decided to boycott lectures from tomorrow, all Federal Universities . . .'

'Until?'

'Until IBB and his khaki-boys get out of the Presidential Villa and . . .'

'That may take long.'

'It'll start tomorrow,' Bola said with the enthusiasm of a kid at a birthday party.

As I lay in the dark, trying to sleep, I felt the dark, lurking figure inching towards the centre.

Now I stood on the verandah, brushing my teeth over the rail. Bola passed me and stood at the head of the two steps that led to the grass below.

'Ants!' he shrieked. I turned, alarmed at the near hysteria in his voice. He was pointing at a long column of black ants passing below the steps. I had never seen them so thickly profuse before. But it was the start of the rainy season, their period for migration.

'They are migrating,' I said, rinsing my mouth. Bola stood there, rooted, staring at them. He turned to me, and now there was renewed urgency in his movements and words.

'You don't understand,' he said.

'What?'

'Something is terribly wrong somewhere.'

'Of course, everything is wrong everywhere,' I said lightly, alarmed by his behaviour. He rushed past me into the room. I found him hastily dressing.

'Where are you going to? You need rest . . .'

'I am going home.' He hopped over to me, one leg in his trousers. He held my arm tightly. 'You don't take me seriously, do you? Something is wrong. I know it. Let's go. Come with me, please.' He sounded desperate. I began to dress without a word; we had been room-mates and close friends for three semesters, and I had never seen Bola this way before. He had his silly moments, his pranks, but never like this. If he goes home and sees that all is well with his parents and sisters he'll calm down, I thought. Besides, his father was a doctor; he'd give him tranquillizers, or something, for his nerves. When we finished dressing we made for the gates, passing students arguing in the centre of the road, some already brandishing placards. Slogans and handbills fluttered in the air to fall like dead leaves on the tarred road. Bola was already out of the gates, running. I hurried to catch up with him. We didn't wait for the bus — we took the first taxi that came.

'Ikeja,' Bola said and entered. I sat beside him. The bags were thick under his rheumy eyes, and I could hear his teeth chattering.

'Everything will be fine, you'll see,' I said, patting his arm, trying to force a smile. I couldn't. I stared out of the window at the walls and billboards flying past by the roadside, most of them defaced with anti-military slogans: 'IBB MUST GO!'; 'NO MORE SOJA!'

More than once our taxi was forced to hug the kerb as siren-blaring military jeeps passed at top speed, gun-toting soldiers hanging recklessly from the rails in the open back.

The Akinyeles lived in Tolani Estate, a Federal Government housing project, in Ikeja. As we approached the house, we saw a red Honda parked in the driveway. Mr Akinyele's car was a white Peugeot 505.

'I wonder whose car that is,' Bola whispered. Then we heard the cries. Women crying. That was when Bola's legs failed him. He sat down abruptly on the concrete ledge circling the verandah. He was sweating freely now; when he looked at me I saw deep terror in his eyes. I sat beside him and put my arm round his shoulders. He was shivering. At last he rallied his courage and stood up. We went in.

The cries stopped when we entered. All movement ceased, all eyes fixed on us, as if we were ghosts. There were six people in the room. I recognized two of them. Auntie Rosa was seated on the sofa, sandwiched between two other women who held her arms, restraining her, whispering consoling words to her — their eyes were all wet with tears. Two men were seated on single seats, facing the women, their hands clasped and hanging between their knees. One was white-haired; his thick glasses flashed as he raised his eyes to look at us. The other man was younger; I had seen the blinking-eyed, tight-lipped face before, in front of one of the neighbouring houses. Uncle Bode was standing. He was Auntie Rosa's husband, Bola's uncle — his father's younger brother. He lived in Ibadan with his family.

He had been pacing; now he stood in mid-stride, one hand in his pocket, staring at us. 'Bola,' he said.

His voice was the cue for Auntie Rosa to give a long, drawn-out wail and jump to her feet. She flew into Bola's arms. 'My child, my poor child,' she sobbed over and over again. Bola stood with his arms around her, his perplexed gaze on her husband. The other women resumed their wailing.

'Bola,' Uncle Bode repeated and stepped forward. He was tall and gawky — the sleeves of his shirt and the legs of his trousers were always too short — like a teenager turning into a man. His face looked more than usually gaunt; a day's stubble covered his cheeks. He pulled his wailing wife gently out of Bola's arms and handed her back to the two women. 'Bola, we sent Paul and Peter to your school. Did they meet you?'

He had a deep voice. He was a barrister. I had met him and his wife once, during the last vacation, which I spent here with Bola's family. Paul and Peter were twins, the couple's only children. They were my age mates, twenty-two, a year older than Bola. Uncle Bode had married earlier than Doctor Akinyele, who had to finish medical school before marrying.

'I . . . we didn't meet,' Bola said. I was standing behind a chair; I could see Bola's profile tensing and relaxing as he tried to maintain a calm countenance. But I imagined his heart galloping like a horse's hooves.

'We sent them to call you . . .' Uncle Bode began; he stopped, as if at a loss what further to say. He turned suddenly to the two men seated with their heads bowed. He pointed to the one with grey hair and said, 'You know Doctor Dimeji, don't you? He works with . . .'

'Yes, Uncle, I know him. But . . . where's Dad and Mum?'

There was a loud silence in the room. The women looked up sharply, their mouths petrified in silent 'O's.

Uncle Bode opened his mouth and closed it again wordlessly. I could see the pain etched like gullies in the landscape of his face; he seemed on the verge of tears. Doctor Dimeji stood up and whispered something into his ear; he nodded vigorously. He turned to Bola and said, 'Let us go to your room. We'll talk there. You too. Bola's friend?'

'Yes, sir,' I said.

I followed them down the corridor to Bola's room. Bola took out his keys and opened the door. The moment we entered, Bola turned and faced his uncle. In a firm voice he said, 'Uncle, I am not a kid. I know something terrible has happened to Dad, or Mum, or both. That's why I came. I knew they were going to you in Ibadan yesterday . . . Has there been . . . an accident?'

The uncle sighed and bowed his head. He appeared relieved that the burden of breaking whatever bad news he carried had been lifted off his shoulders. In a toneless, droning voice he narrated the woeful tale.

There had been an accident. Bola's family — father, mother and two sisters — had been in a car crash. It was late in the evening, yesterday, Wednesday; they were on their way to Ibadan for a visit. The after-rain road was treacherous and full of illusory reflections. The father, driving, had failed to see the truck lying on its side in the middle of the road. It was a military truck carrying the furniture of an officer on transfer from Lagos to Ibadan. The father and mother, who were in front, had died instantly; Peju, the oldest sister, died on the way to the hospital; the other sister, Lola, sustained minor injuries and was presently in a hospital in Ibadan. Uncle Bode had been contacted early this morning by the hospital where Bola's father worked, and the first thing he did after taking the corpses to the mortuary and putting Lola in a good hospital was to bring his wife and children down to Lagos to meet Bola, because he didn't have the courage to do it alone.

'We want you to come with us to Ibadan. Can you?' he asked at the end.

'Of course, of course. I have to see Lola,' Bola replied. His voice was too cordial. His eyes were too bright — but there were no tears in them. He went with stilted steps to the bed and sat down. I sat down beside him. The uncle went and opened the window; he stood with hands folded behind him, his eyes fixed on Bola. I noticed his lips twitching. Bola was staring straight before him at the poster of a musician on the wall. Unseeing. A car came to a stop outside.

'They are back. Paul and Peter. I'll tell them you are here,' Uncle Bode said, but he didn't move.

Bola looked up at him and said in the same cordial voice, 'They must have missed us by minutes.'

'I'll tell them you are here.'

Now we were alone. I didn't know what to say. Anything I said would be inadequate, awkward. Bola was still staring at the poster. The picture had been taken on stage; the man had a microphone in his right hand, close to his mouth. He stared back at us; the red light above him made his hair fiery, like a burning halo.

I cleared my voice. 'The dream you had was right, then,' I said. My voice sounded hollow.

Bola nodded. He was sitting straight, propping himself with both hands on the bed. 'Just like that.'

I wished he would cry, or scream. This calm was unnatural. 'I am sorry . . .'

'Thank you,' he replied automatically. I was relieved when the uncle returned with Peter and Paul in tow. They formed a solemn line, the father in the centre, facing us. The twins — huge and awkward, politely smiling and looking sad all at once — were so identical it was impossible to distinguish one from the other.

'Peter, Paul,' Bola intoned with a bright smile. 'You missed us.'

'Yes,' they both replied.

'We found the campus gate barred by the students — there was a sort of demonstration going on,' the twin on the father's left added.

'So they've already started,' Bola said, turning to me. There was a long silence.

The uncle put his hands in his pockets and brought them out again. He caught my eye. 'Let me have a word with you,' he said and walked out. He was waiting for me in the corridor. 'Well, what do you think? Isn't he behaving strangely?'

I nodded. 'Yes. Maybe we should call the doctor.'

'Good. Go and call him.'

I went to the living room. The women looked up expectantly when I entered.

'How is he? How is the poor boy?' Auntie Rosa asked between sobs.

'He is fine.'

I looked at the two men who were still in the same posture as before, hunched forward in their seats, their hands clasped between their knees.

'Uncle Bode wants a word with you, Doctor.'

Uncle Bode met us halfway down the corridor. 'I think you need to take a look at him, Doctor. He appears too composed, too calm. Not a single tear.'

'It is normal. He is in deep shock, too shocked to cry. The tears will come later,' the doctor said. 'The best thing now is for him to rest. Let me get my bag.'

When he returned, he gave Bola an injection in the arm. Bola extended his arm and stared at the needle disappearing into his flesh without flinching. The doctor patted him on the shoulder. 'That will make you sleep. You need the rest.'

'Thank you,' Bola said.

'You'll stay with him,' the doctor told me as they all left.

Bola stood up and undressed to his boxer shorts and inner vest. 'I am groggy already,' he said.

I cleared the bed and waved him into it. He fell asleep almost immediately. The morning was still fresh; my watch said ten o'clock. But I felt so weary, as if I had not slept for days. I got up and began to pace the room, stopping to stare at Bola whenever he shifted. His mouth was open. He snored. His brows were knitted, as if he was trying to make sense of all that had happened, even as he slept.

MY FRIEND, MY friend. How I wish I could ease your pain somehow.

The first time we met, over a year ago, we were both freshmen. He was immediately behind me in the queue for accommodation. Somehow we discovered that we were both in Theatre Arts. And when he discovered that I was not from Lagos, he immediately adopted me.

'We'll stay in the same room. You need a Lagosian like me to show you what time it is, you know what 'am saying?' he said in his best American accent.

And before two weeks were over, he had introduced me to his family. 'My northern friend,' he said. So trusting, so guileless, so loyal. I started spending my vacations with his family after the first semester.

'What are you going back to the North for? Ain't nothing happening there but goats and cows and deserts. Chill, man, chill.'

His mother and sisters joined in to persuade me. From then on I found I had a home from home, another family.

THE DOCTOR APPEARED suddenly at the door, his bag in his hand.

'He won't wake up soon,' he said, staring at Bola. Then he blinked at me behind his thick spectacles and asked, 'Were they close, the family?'

I pondered the question for a while, jolted by his use of the past tense. Perhaps he wanted a reason why Bola had not cried.

'Very close, all of them.'

When he left, I pulled out a chair from the reading table and sat at the window, staring out. Brightly coloured birds flitted about in the frangipani bush behind the neighbouring house. They chirped merrily to each other. They were picking straw to build their nests. Their movements were jerky, sharp. They looked so vital, so frenzied, as if in a rush to burn out their short, avian lives, as if trying to get it all over with before the evil shape lurking in the darkness emerged fully.

Now I could hear voices from the living room — male voices, deep and restrained: the twins and their father and the other man. The doctor had left. And renewed wailing from the women. One of them stopped wailing and began to lament in a lilting, singsong voice. When I closed my eyes, and my mind, the voice could be that of Ma Bola. But it was only my fancy playing. She was dead, lying beside her husband and pretty eighteen-year-old Peju, who had wanted to be a presenter on TV.

I must have drifted off to sleep, my head on my arms on the window ledge. One of the twins woke me up with a plate of rice. It was three in the afternoon.

'Daddy's gone to Ibadan, to be with Lola,' he said. I took the plate of rice and kept it on the floor. I was not hungry.

'We are all going to meet him tomorrow — with Bola.'

'Paul, do you . . .' I began, but he interrupted me with a smile and said, 'Peter.'

'Sorry.'

'It is OK. Even Dad has trouble with that sometimes. What were you saying?'

I had forgotten what I wanted to say, so I asked, 'Did you see Lola? She wasn't badly injured, was she?'

'She wasn't, just shocked. She was unconscious.' That meant she might not be aware of her parents' and sister's death. I lowered my head, thinking of the pain waiting to spring upon her. Bola turned and kicked a leg and muttered.

'The doctor said he won't wake up till tomorrow,' Peter said.

After a while he left me and returned to the living room. I pictured him and his brother seated at the dining table, staring without appetite into their plates of rice. The red stew would appear like blood to them, and the white mound of rice beneath it like . . . like brain matter, perhaps, scooped out of a wide-open skull. When my legs grew heavy from sitting, I got out of the room and took the back door, through the kitchen, to the backyard. I paced for a while on the grass, smoking a cigarette, keeping close to Bola's window, an ear cocked for the slightest sound. When I got tired of pacing I sat down on the soak-away pit slab, watching the birds watching me warily as they went about their straw picking.

We slept early. At seven o'clock, before turning in, Auntie Rosa and the twins came in to say good night. I was seated on the chair, staring through the window at the darkness outside. I turned and stood up. We watched as she went and stood at the edge of the bed, her hands clasped over her bosom. She remained like that for almost ten minutes, staring at Bola's sprawled form. Then she turned to us. Her face looked tired, her eyes were red and swollen. She raised up her hands, her face staring at the ceiling. 'God, God, it is you that knows everything,' she said, her voice husky and cracked from crying.

'Good night, we are in the living room if you need us,' Paul and Peter chorused as they led their mother away.

BOLA WOKE UP around three a.m. I had not slept; I had lain in the dark, staring at the ceiling through the gloom. Different thoughts flitted through my mind as I listened to his heavy breathing beside me. Then the breathing stopped abruptly. He sat up. I felt him staring at me. I held my breath, my eyes shut tight, pretending to be asleep. He got out of bed, feeling his way carefully in the dark. He went out of the room. Through the half-open door I heard his soft footsteps heading for the bathroom. When he returned he stood in the dark facing me, then he went and turned on the light. Through slitted eyes I watched him take out something from the desk drawer — it was his photo album. He moved the chair to the desk and opened the album and started to flip through the pages. It was his family album. I knew the pictures, each and every one of them. On my first night in this room, we had lain on this bed, side by side, as he turned the pages and introduced me to each snapshot, each occasion, each universe. I gritted my teeth and shut my eyes tight as I felt the tears threatening to overflow. Not now, Lord.

MY FIRST DAY with the family replayed itself in my mind, but in black and white, and the reel grainy and distorted in places. I was seated with the family, nervous, pretending to follow Carl Sagan on TV, covertly assessing their movements and utterances. Peju, seated next to me, suddenly turned and asked casually, 'Lomba, what is the capital of Iceland?'

I discovered later that she was going to read journalism at the university and ultimately become a presenter on CNN. She had stacks of cassette recordings of herself reading the news in a cool, assured voice. I looked at her blankly. She was seventeen, and her beauty was just starting to extricate itself from the awkward, pimply encumbrances of adolescence. Her eyes were polite but unrelentingly expectant. Surprised at the question, not knowing the answer, I turned to Bola for help — but he was lost in a loud and argumentative game of *Ludo* with his mum on the carpet. I shrugged and smiled. 'Why would I know what the capital of Iceland is?'

'Good answer, Lomba,' came the father's voice from behind the *Sunday Guardian*. He was lying on the sofa; he had been listening to us all along.

'Stay out, Daddy,' Peju pleaded, and turning back to me she proceeded to lecture me on the name and geographical peculiarities of Reykjavik. The next salvo came from Lola, who was going to be a fashion designer. She was twelve and intimidatingly precocious. She had sidled up to me and sat on the arm of my seat, listening innocently to Peju's lecture; but as soon as it was over she took my arm and gave me a cherubic smile. 'Do you know how a bolero jacket looks?'

When I replied, naturally, in the negative, she jumped up gleefully and ran to their room and came back with her sketchbook and a pencil. She dragged me down to the carpet and quickly sketched a bolero jacket for me. I stared in silence at the tiny hand so sure behind the pencil, and the wispy but exact strokes slowly arranging themselves into a distinct shape.

'The tailor is making one for me. You'll see it when it is ready,' she promised.

'What do you use it for?'

'To dance the bolero — it is a Spanish dance.'

'Can you dance it?'

'No, but I'll learn.'

'You'll wear him out with your nonsense, girls,' the father said, standing up and stretching. He yawned. 'Time for my siesta.' He left.

At first I was discomfited by his taciturnity, which I mistook for moodiness; but in close-up I saw the laughter kinks behind the eyes, the lips twitching, ready to part and reveal the white teeth beneath. I came to discover his playful side, his pranks on the girls, his comradely solidarity with Bola against the others. Apart from his work, his family was his entire life. Now I saw him — in black and white — after work, at home, seated on his favourite sofa, watching CNN or reading the papers, occasionally turning to answer Lola's persistent, needling questions, or to explain patiently to Bola why he couldn't afford to buy him a new pair of sneakers just now. Big, gentle, quiet, speaking only when spoken to. Remember him: conscientious doctor, dutiful father, loving husband and, to me, a perfect role model.

But Ma Bola was my favourite, perhaps because she was so different from my mother, who was, coincidentally, the same age as her. Ma Bola was slim, her figure unaltered by years of childbirth.

'Your sister?' people often asked Bola, and he'd look at his mother and they'd laugh before correcting the mistake. Ma Bola was a secretary at the Ministry of Finance — she called her husband 'darling', like white people. Her children were 'dear' or 'honey'. The first time she called me that, I turned round to see if there was someone else behind me. She had laughed and patted me on the cheek. 'Don't worry, you'll get used to our silly ways.' Like white people. Her greatest charm was her ease with people. She laughed so easily; she listened with so much empathy, patting you on the arm to make a point. After a minute with her you were a captive for life.

'Take care of my husband for me,' she told me often. That was how she sometimes fondly referred to Bola: 'my husband'. 'He can be so impulsive, so exasperatingly headstrong.'

'I will,' I promised.

She went on to tell me how, in traditional society, parents used to select friends for their children. We were alone in the kitchen. She was teaching me how to make pancakes. 'Cousins, usually. They'd select someone of opposite temperament — someone quiet, if theirs was garrulous, someone level-headed (like you), if their own was impulsive. They'd make them sworn friends for life, to check each other's excesses. Very wise, don't you think?'

'Very.'

'If I was to select a friend for Bola, it'd be you. But Providence has already done it for me.'

Bola. He was the centre of the house, spoilt silly by them all. He could make even a stone laugh with his crazy antics. He was a gust of wind, a stream of raw energy tearing through the recumbent house whenever he came home for weekends: overturning chairs as he chased Peju or Lola to the haven of their father's arms; opening pots and drawers in the kitchen.

He was something different to each one of them. To the father, he was the heir to be nurtured with a judicious mixture of love, severity, distance, closeness, manly camaraderie, and sometimes a helpless burst of fondness so touching to see. To Ma Bola he was the love of her life, her man renewed all over again, but this time as the flesh of her own flesh. To the girls he was the other, the male, through whom they could vent their curiosity about that increasingly alluring world of boys, without fear of being singed.

As the reel came to an end, just before the credits, I saw the truck, close-up, in the centre of the road, the small family car coalesced to its exposed bowels. The blood, in black and white, was not red but black. Thick and viscous. At last the creature had come out to take a bow. Fade to black and chaos.

WHEN I WOKE up two and a half hours later, I was alone. Bola's jeans and shirt were there on the table where I had placed them last night. He would be in the toilet, or the kitchen. I sat on the edge of the bed and watched the weak morning rays buffeting motes in their stream. The birds were chirping outside, as if all was well with the world. After fifteen minutes I went to the toilet. I knocked and entered. It was empty. I went to the kitchen. It was empty. I hesitated before the master bedroom at the head of the corridor. When I tried the door it was locked.

Auntie Rosa and the women from yesterday were in the girls' room, opposite Bola's room, but he wouldn't be there. I decided to wake up the twins. Paul — or was it Peter? — was on the sofa, on his back, one leg and one arm dangling over the edge and on to the carpet. His brother was on the carpet, on three cushions that he must have carefully arranged in a straight row before sleeping, but which were now scattered around him. I checked the front door before waking them up; it was locked. They looked at me without comprehension, their brains groggy from sleep, when I told them I couldn't find Bola.

'Check the toilet. He must be in the toilet,' Paul said when at last my words registered.

'I've checked.'

'And the kitchen, everywhere?'

I nodded. They both turned to stare at the locked front door. Paul went to wake up his mother while I went to check the back door. The door was shut, but when I turned the handle it opened. I stared at the narrow path between the dewy morning grass, leading to a wider path that met the tarred road that led to the Estate gates.

'The back door is open,' I said superfluously when they joined me.

Auntie Rosa brushed past me to stand in the grass outside, wringing her hands, looking up and down. Her eyes were red from yesterday's tears and from lack of sleep. Her face sagged, lumpy, like clay. Her head was bare, her hair unkempt.

'Where could he have gone to? Was he dressed? Does he have close friends around that he might have gone to? But why, so early in the morning, and without telling anyone?' she poured out, speaking more to herself than to anyone else. I could see her lips quivering. Soon she'd start crying.

'Let me get my shoes, then we'll go to his friend's house,' I said to the twins.

But Muyiwa was away at school. His father stood at the door, blinking suspiciously at us. He was in shorts; his legs were thick and hairy.

'You say you are Bola's cousins? Why are you looking for him so early, didn't he sleep at home?'

'He did. He went out and we have to travel with him to Ibadan now,' Paul improvised lamely.

We checked two more houses that I knew, but all in vain. On the way back to the house, Peter stopped suddenly and called after us, 'What are we going to tell her?'

We turned back and took the road to the gate. The Estate was coming awake slowly. Boys washed their parents' cars outside the houses; dogs stretched their stiff limbs before the front doors. At the gates, I stopped at the Meigad's shed and asked him in Hausa if he had seen Bola. Bola often stopped at the man's stall to sneak a cigarette and try a newly acquired Hausa word before passing.

'Yes,' the man replied in his halting English. 'Now now he pass. He is wear am short knickers.'

We hurried up the road where the Meigad had pointed.

'But where could he be going to?' Paul asked wretchedly. We were almost running now. Market women with wares huddled in baskets before them waited at bus stops beside civil servants clutching thick folders, their broad neckties hanging before them like weights, bending them forward. Peter saw the crowd first, about a kilometre from the Estate gates.

'What's that?' he muttered. A small crowd ahead, by the roadside. But crowds are a normal aspect of Lagos streets: bell-ringing commodity hawkers offering a bargain, or a miracle healer plying his trade, or a fight, or a robber being lynched, or a preacher . . . It was a preacher. He was balanced precariously on an upturned bin, arms flailing demonstratively as he sang a song of devotion preparatory to a sermon.

It was not a preacher, it was Bola. We stood at the crowd's fringe, staring, dumbfounded. The song was 'Onward Christian Soldiers', and his chest heaved and his eyes rolled with fanatical frenzy as he sang it. He was barefooted, dressed only in his boxer shorts and a flimsy T-shirt. He stopped the song abruptly mid-stanza and began to speak.

'The military has failed us. I say down with khakistocracy! Down with militocracy! Down with kleptocracy!' His right hand, clenched in a fist, pumped up and down with each declamation. 'According to Wole Soyinka, "The man dies in him who stands silent in the face of tyranny." According to Amilcar Cabral . . .'

He was repeating, word for word, Sankara's speech of yesterday.

'Something is wrong with him,' Paul said, shock and dismay in his voice. 'He is foaming at the mouth.'

He must have been at it for some time now. He looked exhausted, but he was gripped by some maniacal energy that kept him standing, waving his arms, pushing his progressively hoarsening voice to the edge of the gathering and beyond. The crowd consisted mainly of loafers: park touts, out-of-work bus conductors, Area Boys, all eager for a little diversion, drawn by the acrid whiff of incipient violence. The respectable part of the crowd, civil servants on their way to work, began to disperse as Bola's words became more and more incendiary.

'Let's get him,' I said to the twins. I began to push forward. 'Excuse me please, excuse me.' I ignored the glares and hisses, firmly pushing aside elbows and shoulders. Peter and Paul followed closely in my wake. When we were almost at the centre, we suddenly realized that we were not the only ones approaching Bola. Two men, identically dressed in long black coats and dark glasses, had reached him just a step ahead of us. One was talking to him; one stood beside him, his eyes panning the crowd, his hands in his pockets. Security agents.

'Bola!' Peter called. At the sound of his name, Bola lifted his eyes and began to smile. But the men held both his arms and plucked him down from his perch. He followed them meekly as they forced their way through the crowd. We hurried after them till we were walking abreast of them.

'Excuse me, please,' I began, but they neither looked at me nor faltered in their determined progress to a black Peugeot 504 with tinted windows parked by the roadside. As they approached, the back door opened and another black-clad, glasses-wearing figure stepped out and dragged Bola into the car, shutting the door after him. Now the two men turned and faced us; there was a large crowd behind us. They stood so that they blocked the car door, their hands in their coat pockets.

'Please,' I began, and stopped. I didn't know what more to say. If only I could see their eyes, but their glasses were like walls separating them from us.

'You can't take him away!' Peter interjected. 'He is our brother! He is not well.'

'He is not well,' Paul echoed.

'Please.'

Now one of them opened his mouth to a trap-like slit and hissed, 'Get lost if you know what is good for you.'

'You don't understand . . .' I began desperately, but before I could say more a stone whizzed past me from behind and exploded on the car's windscreen. The two men ducked instinctively.

'Thieves!'

'Ole!'

'Give them their brother, government boy-boy!'

I saw the men straighten up, their hands whipping out of their pockets simultaneously. I turned and followed the scattering crowd as I saw the guns. Shots rang in the air; the figure before me fell, I tripped over it and fell too, bruising my knees and elbows badly. When I got up the car was driving away. Some of the Area Boys were chasing after it, emptily cursing and throwing stones at its fast-disappearing back. Paul came and gave me his hand; I took it and stood up.

'They are gone,' he said. 'They've taken him away.' He spoke as if he couldn't believe what had happened; as if hoping I'd contradict him. But I couldn't. I nodded. He sat down abruptly, right there by the road. He held his head in his hands.

'What are we going to do now?' he said over and over. I looked around for Peter. I saw him coming from across the road; he was panting hard. 'What are we going to do now?' Paul repeated to him dully.

'We'll phone Daddy. I've got their car number.' His voice tried hard to be optimistic. 'Daddy will know what to do.'

I nodded. Paul stood up and we headed for the Estate gates.

THE NEXT DAY, in the evening, I returned to the university hostels. I walked slowly through the gates, lost in thought. Thoughts that converged in a confused, convoluted mass, then slowly receded, frittering away to nothingness. Flooding and ebbing, chafing at the seams of my sanity.

As I neared my block, I began to notice how quiet and deserted everywhere looked. I had not passed a single student since I entered the gates; the basketball court, the kiosks, the benches, all were empty. Something was wrong. I remembered the boycott of lectures, the promised demonstration. I had been away for two days, and in that space anything could have happened. The air everywhere was so volatile, so charged, waiting to explode. I saw two boys standing at the turning to the girls' blocks. They had stopped talking and were staring at me. I raised my hand and waved. They waved back.

My room was open, the door broken, hanging askew from the top hinge, half-blocking the entrance. And there were papers scattered all over the verandah and the steps, down to the grass. I looked around: other doors stood open, revealing empty interiors. I followed the trail of papers into the room. The room looked as if a battle had been fought in it: the mattresses were thrown on the floor; books, papers, file binders and cups and spoons covered the space around the mattresses, looking like motifs in a demented collage. I picked up a paper from the floor; it was a poem, my poem. I picked up another; it was a page from one of my short stories. I looked at the other papers, recognizing my handwriting, scared to bend down and gather them. Most of them were torn; boots had marched upon them, covering the writing with thick, brown mud. I felt the imprint of the boots on my mind; I felt the rifling, tearing hands ripping through my very soul. All I could think of as I stood there, with the torn, mud-caked papers in my hands and around me, was: I have been writing these stories and poems for as long as I can remember now, these are my secret thoughts and dreams.

I sat on the naked bedsprings. I saw my bag in a corner; shirt-sleeves and trouser-legs trailed out of it like intestines from a busted carcass. My mind was sore, tired; I could not think. The sound of feet shuffling up and down in the next room made me stand up. I rushed out. It was Adegbite. He was in the middle of the room, bending over an open box. He was stuffing books and clothes indiscriminately into it. He turned when he heard my footsteps. His eyes were wide and scared. He laughed when he saw me.

'Lomba! Man, I thought it was the fucking police again.'

'Police?'

'Yes. Where have you been? You missed the action. It was bloody brilliant.'

I looked round the room. Here, also, the mattresses were on the floor, and the iron window was broken off its hinges — that was all. No torn papers.

'It began on Thursday,' Adegbite said. 'You were here, weren't you? We were stopped in the streets, halfway to the military governor's house. We were going there to stage a peaceful demonstration, that was all. They appeared from nowhere in their trucks, shooting tear gas and rubber bullets at us. At first we scattered, but we rallied ourselves and returned. They were not much, just a truckful of them — about thirty persons. We broke their windscreen with stones, and we also seized their truck, but reinforcement came for them, this time with real bullets. One student was shot in the leg. When we saw the leg shattered and bloody we decided to call it a day. But the bastards followed us to the hostels, chased us to our rooms. The air was so thick with tear gas we couldn't breathe. They went from room to room, breaking doors and looting. When we heard the girls scream-ing 'rape!', our courage was rekindled. You should've seen Sankara directing us at the basketball court, like a fucking general. We soaked our handkerchiefs in kerosene and tied them over our noses to neutralize the tear gas. We made petrol bombs — then we advanced to the girls' hostels. Tak-ing cover from block to block. Running across the open spaces. They started firing when they saw us coming, but that crazy guy Sankara ran right at them, two flaming bottles in his hands. He hurled the bottles at their truck and it caught fire. That really made them mad. They flushed us out of the hostels into the streets. But that was to our advantage, because the Area Boys and park touts soon joined our ranks. Christ, it was brilliant. The street was like a fucking war zone, filled with smoke and darting figures and fire and gunshots. One student died. He was shot in the head — a chemistry student. The Area Boys captured a policeman and doused him in petrol and set him ablaze. More policemen came — that was when I decided it was not safe to stay. I escaped through the back streets. Later, we heard on the radio that all students should pack out of the hostels. The school was closed. We also heard that Sankara and two others were taken by the police. It is only today that I worked up the courage to come and pack my things. Man, it was bloody.'

'Our room has been broken into.'

'Yeah, I saw it. A great mess. I saw this bag there, untouched. I was going to drop it with the porters. Is it yours?' He pointed to it under the table — zipped and locked.

'It is Bola's bag.'

'Where is he?'

'He . . . he couldn't come,' I said. 'I'll take it to him.' I picked up the bag and started out.

'Hey, wait for me. Let's leave together. Give me five minutes.'

'OK. Meet me when you are through.'

Back in my room, I put the bag down and began to collect my poems and stories from the floor. I just couldn't leave them lying around like that, my own creations. I found their folder, torn, under a mattress. I followed the trail of papers to the verandah and the courtyard. I gathered them in a pile on the grass and set fire to them. My eyes filled with tears as I watched the pages curl and blacken in the flames.

As we walked to the gates, Adegbite kept pointing out to me particular spots and little memorials of the battle with the police. A broken bottle, a shattered kiosk, a busted window. I listened without speaking, my mind filled with other thoughts. Bola would be in Ibadan by now, with his uncle, Auntie Rosa, and the twins. This morning he had not recognized me. Adegbite shook my hand outside the gates and said, 'See you when we return.' I stood and watched him cross the road and get on a bus. But I was not coming back here. I knew that deep inside.

As I turned and surveyed the gate and the fences beside it, I saw the fences suddenly transform into thick walls, standing tall, top-tufted with barbed wire and broken bottles, arms widespread to restrain and contain and limit. I wanted no more limits; only those I set for myself.

I started down the road, hefting Bola's bag on to my shoulder. I didn't know what to do with the bag. I should have left it with the porters. A bus slowed down and the conductor urged me to hurry up. I started to run after it, and then I stopped. I was not in a hurry to go anywhere because I had nowhere to go. Anti-riot policemen still patrolled on foot, in groups, combing the deserted back streets for trouble, tear-gas canisters hanging from their belts, and rifles from their shoulders. I shivered.

YESTERDAY UNCLE BODE had traced the Peugeot 504 to the divisional office of the State Security Service. After explaining things for over an hour, he had been told to return today. He went back early this morning. He was directed to the psychiatric hospital in Yaba. Later, when we went, Peter, Paul and I, we found him and Auntie Rosa seated glumly beside a hospital bed on which Bola lay, staring at the ceiling.

'See what they did to him,' Auntie Rosa said and burst into tears.

We flinched as our eyes fell on his bare torso: every inch was covered with thick, punctured weals. He had been systematically beaten from his face down to his legs. One arm was fractured — it lay by his side in a thick plaster. And he didn't recognize us. His eyes passed over us incuriously before returning to stare with mindless vacuity at the ceiling.

'See what they have done to him! God will pay them back!' Auntie Rosa cried. Uncle Bode got up and walked out to pace the verandah.

THEY HAD BEATEN him all night, shouting questions at his bewildered, whimpering face. Finally they had realized that something was wrong with him. Disgusted, they had dumped him at the psychiatric hospital.

I didn't stay long with them. I couldn't continue to stare at that silent, blinking form on the bed any longer. I told them I was going back to school. They said they'd take him to Ibadan for traditional treatment. They said they'd let me know when to come for the burial. But now I had no address. I was simply walking down this deserted road with nowhere to go.

ALICE

THE LAST TIME Lomba had seen Alice, she had been walking away from him towards the cancer ward where her mother lay dying. Now she was right here before him, smiling happily up at him in a bridal dress. Someone had placed a full-page notice to announce the happy event — only Alice didn't look that happy. He brought the newspaper closer to his face and peered into the eyes, the lips, the bouquet. The smile from this close was a grimace, the edges of the petals were curling, drying — but it was the eyes that gave him more hope. They told him all he needed to know: that Alice still loved him. They weren't looking at the camera, nor at the groom beside her; they were looking past the camera, beyond it, at the congregation in the church hall, and he had no doubt that it was him she sought.

And when you looked and hoped and waited and finally realized that I was never going to come, that you had just made a final, irrevocable choice — 'I do' — did you not break down and cry?

LIKE THAT DAY when she had walked away from him in the evening gloom towards the cancer ward — she had had tears in her eyes. One thing he knew of her: she wasn't scared of making hard decisions, even if they caused her tears. Was that what had made him want her in the first place? He could not remember now — there was her sheer overpowering beauty, of course, but that was not it. If you knew Alice for an hour you'd know that the beauty wasn't just it. There was something else. What makes art collectors pine and ache with longing the moment they see a rare work they just have to have? But even that, Lomba knew, was a poor analogy. This was soul calling to soul. A tired, trapped lock at last meeting the key that unlocks it.

He had seen her first in a lecturer's office, in his second year of school. He was between lectures, and his favourite place for killing time was Dr Kareem's office. He could spend hours there discussing his poetry with the old lecturer, and at that period in his life there was nothing Lomba preferred than to have his poems discussed and argued; it gave him some kind of vague hope, a sense of place in the larger scheme of things. But he had found Dr Kareem busy with new students. Two girls in the two seats far against the wall, facing the grey-headed lecturer. Lomba had caught him at the homily moment. Good, that meant the registration was over and the girls would soon be gone.

'I'll be back,' Lomba said, by the door.

'No. Come in. I was just telling these latecomers about you. Girls, if I were you, having resumed late, I'd stick close to this young man here. He is the best in your class. Beg him for his notes and take any advice he gives you. Lomba, they are direct-entry students. I leave them in your hands. Show them where they'll pay the departmental fees. I've spoken,' Dr Kareem ended in his characteristic manner.

Lomba turned to the two girls. One was in jeans, her legs crossed. The other was in a skirt; she was seated at the edge of her seat, a quiet, attentive look on her face. A car key dangled from the fingers of one hand, the other hand clutched a bag in her lap.

'Well,' Lomba said and stepped out into the corridor. They had to run to keep up with him as he went down the stairs.

'Don't go so fast,' Jeans whined.

'OK,' Lomba said and stopped abruptly. They bumped into him.

'Oops!'

'Sorry. But you don't need me any more. You can see the building from here.' He pointed. 'Just go through that door and ask for the cash clerk.'

'But the lecturer said you have to take us there . . .' Jeans began.

How young and fresh and foolish she looks, Lomba thought. She had on the same wig all the other girls on campus were wearing, the same tight top, the same faded jeans. One year in school and he already felt jaded and super-annuated.

'I heard what the lecturer said, but I have a lecture to catch. Bye.'

'Bust the lecture.'

Were they the first words I ever heard you utter or were they just the first words that stuck in my mind? I am not certain. But they are words that define you more than any others I can remember. What they did was to make me look at you for the first time; all this while I had only looked at your friend — you had that ability of a cryptic animal to blend into the back-ground, as if you were saving the viewer from the full, shocking impact of your beauty. You were the Medusa. I turned into stone. When I smiled my smile was shaky, when I spoke my words were strangled.

'I don't bust my lectures,' I said and left.

ALICE WAS NOT a serious student. She attended lectures no more than three times in a week. Lomba was not to see her again for over a week. A car came to a stop before the lecture hall and she stepped out. Lomba was standing in front of the hall with a group of students, waiting for the lecturer.

'Wow!' somebody whispered. 'She is coming this way.'

Without thinking, Lomba stepped forward and met her halfway.

'My first day in school,' she said, smiling, taking his hand.

'I am nervous. Let us go and sit there. Is the lecturer here yet?'

They sat on white plastic seats outside a kiosk, in the weak morning sun, drinking Coke. The lecturer came and lectured and left.

'What happened? I thought you had dropped out before you'd even started.'

'I've been looking for a place. My Dad doesn't want me to stay in the hostels. A flat close to school. And you, where do you stay?'

'In the hostels.'

He noticed how boys turned to stare at her as they passed. She was in a trouser suit today, like an office worker. Her black leather shoes matched her handbag. She looked at her watch (gold, he noted) and said, 'The driver will be back soon. Let us walk to the road and wait for him.'

When the car came, he noted that the driver was in army uniform. A General's daughter, he told himself.

WHEN SHE FINALLY got the house, two weeks later, she told him and invited him over.

'Come and have dinner. I'll cook.'

'I love her so much it makes me sick just to stand close to her,' Lomba confessed to Bola on the day of the dinner. He was getting dressed.

'Here, rub on some of this cologne. The trick is to make an impression. Don't appear too eager. Don't raise your voice when you speak to her. Cool, you know what I mean? Let her

bend to you to hear you. Then the cologne will hit her, get it?'
Bola drilled him relentlessly. 'T-shirt! Please, how can you
wear a T-shirt to a first date? Take my blazer, there is more
attitude to that.'

'But it is hot.'

'And so? Do you want to impress her or not? Wear it, you
can take it off in her room, but remember to take it off only
as you are about to sit down. For maximum effect.'

Lomba did not bother to ask why removing the blazer at
the point of sitting down would lend the gesture maximum
effect. Bola was full of such crazy affectations. Lomba was
too busy rehearsing in his mind what to say to Alice.

Her flat was not too far from the hostels; Lomba took a
footpath through a torn portion of the campus fence and he
was soon there. The house was a two-bedroom brick building
hidden behind a tall wall, like most of the other houses in the
quiet residential area. He pushed open an ornamented iron
gate and entered the compound. She has visitors, he thought,
disappointment washing over him, when he saw a green sports
car parked outside the front door. Music blared through the
open door. He rang the doorbell. He heard voices, laughter.
Male and female.

'Come in, the door is open,' the female voice called. He
pushed aside the curtain and went in. It was not Alice. He
felt relieved and happy, he couldn't tell why. It was a tall, thin
girl in hipsters and T-shirt. She was slouched in her seat, her
legs on a side table before her. A cigarette burned in her
hand. A man was seated beside her, a mulatto with a crew
cut. He looked at Lomba and turned to the girl, who flicked
ashes from her cigarette and asked, 'Yes, can I help you?' Her

voice was hoarse, as if she had a cold. She had a thin, hungry face.

'I came to see Alice,' he said, wondering for a moment if he was in the wrong place.

'Sit down, she will be out in a minute.'

Did Lomba imagine it, or did the man frown when he mentioned Alice? He sat down; he did not remember to remove his blazer for effect. The music was coming from a video of a musical. He watched the figures on the TV screen jump and prance without really hearing the words. The mulatto had some kind of affected foreign accent: American, nasal and unnatural, like those cowboys in films. The girl laughed loudly at whatever joke he was making. Lomba looked at her when she began to cough after a bout of laughter. Her bony frame wracked and shook, she held a hand to her chest, gasping for breath, her eyes ran with tears. The man looked pleased with himself. Lomba wondered who they were. He had never seen their faces before — maybe they were not students, maybe they had come together to visit Alice . . .

'Wow, stunning! Come! Come and give us a kiss!' the mulatto shouted theatrically, spreading wide his arms, his eyes on the passage behind Lomba. Alice had appeared. She did look stunning; she was dressed for going out, most likely to a party: a very short miniskirt, a body-hugging top underneath a red blazer; her red handbag trailed from her hand negligently. She looked self-conscious. The man stood up and engulfed her in his arms; he planted a deep, wet kiss on her lips.

'Alice, someone to see you,' the other girl announced. In

his confusion and discomfort, Lomba noticed that the girl sounded churlish, piqued, like a child who had been suddenly upstaged by the arrival of another. Still in the man's arms, Alice looked over her shoulder at Lomba.

'My classmate, Lomba,' she introduced. 'This is Mike, and this is Nike, my flatmate.'

Lomba smiled at everyone.

The next semester when I saw you knocking on my door, I had a mind to turn and walk away. I stood a long time on the verandah of the opposite block debating. I knew if I came to you, if I called your name, if I let you into my room, nothing would ever be the same again. Why did I hesitate? Was this not what I had wanted ever since the day I first saw you in Dr Kareem's office — to be entangled with you, to twine my life around yours like vine around a post? But I was hesitant, because now I knew there were other dimensions to you that I had never guessed at, that I had only glimpsed the day you left me with your flatmate and walked out with your boyfriend. I had avoided you from that day, treated you like any other classmate, hiding the ache in my heart, the way my heart leaped each time you walked into class . . . Now you were knocking on my door. I could turn, I could walk away; but like a moth approaching a flame, I fluttered to you.

'Alice,' Lomba called. She had raised her hand to knock again when he called. He saw the relief on her face when she turned and saw him.

'Lomba, I was just about to go. I was passing and I stopped to say hi,' she said, trying to sound cool. He opened the door and asked her in. The room looked scattered, as he and his room-mate had left it in the morning: dirty teacups on the table, papers on the floor, the radio still on. He opened the window and let in the hot air and the weak evening light.

'We left in a rush this morning. We were late for 202.' He pulled out the chair next to the table for her — the only chair in the room. 'Sit down. You are not in a hurry to leave, are you? Sit down, let me get you a Coke.'

He was flustered. He wanted to be away from her, he wanted to organize his thoughts. 'OK,' she said and sat down.

When he came back, she was nodding to the song on the radio, softly singing along. She had turned up the volume. He sat on the bed, half-facing her. He kept the Coke on the table beside the radio, beside her handbag. Her legs were crossed. He wanted to ask her where she had been — he had not seen her in class for over two weeks.

He said, 'Your Coke.'

'Thanks.'

He wanted to ask her why she had bags under her eyes, why she looked thinner, unhappy.

'Diana Ross,' he said. 'You like her?'

'My favourite, "Upside Down".'

'I prefer "Endless Love", with Lionel Ritchie. But she can't sing like Millie Jackson, or Betty Wright.'

'I disagree. She has more class.'

'But less soul.' He wanted to ask why she was here today.

She said, 'My father's favourites are Sam Cooke and Otis Redding. I grew up listening to them. My father was just crazy about soul music. He bought stacks of their records when he was in America . . . I have them now. He gave them to me, complete with the turntable. I guess he is a bit too old for soul music now.' She laughed.

'You never get too old for good music.'

There was silence. The atmosphere became a bit heavy; the magic that had animated it a moment ago had fizzled out.

Lomba picked a magazine up from the table and opened it. 'My write-up, it came out last week.' He handed her the magazine.

'"The Military in Nigerian Politics",' she read the title. 'My father is a soldier.'

'I know. I am not condemning them all.'

'That is not what I mean,' she said, shaking her head.

'What do you mean?' He was being obstinate and childish, he knew, but he could not help it. After all, it was she who had come knocking on his door.

'I just wanted to see you and maybe say sorry for the other day,' she said. She gulped down half of her drink, picked up her bag and stood up. 'Now I have to go.'

He stood up. She had not moved from her position, so they were face to face. She was the same height as him. He marvelled at the pure white of her eyes.

Now she turned and made for the door. 'Maybe after today you won't avoid me so much in class,' she threw over her shoulder.

He stood and watched her back till she reached the door. All he could think of was that he had been given an opening for God knows what reason, and he had bungled it. If only he had the guts, he'd reach out and pull her back and crush her lips with his. He gulped the rest of her Coke and followed her outside.

'If you are going back to your place, you don't have to take a bus, there is a path through the fence that takes you there in about ten minutes. Let me show you.' He led the way and she followed without a word.

They took the path through the torn portion in the fence. On the way they tried to make small talk, but without success.

'I never knew this short cut existed,' she said.

'I discovered it the day I went to your place,' he replied.

They fell silent after that. Soon they were in front of the ornamented iron gate.

'Here we are,' he announced proudly, like a genie that had conjured up some wonderful spectacle for her delight alone.

'Well, come on in and listen to some of my soul records — I have lots and lots of them,' she said, and pushed open the gate before he could comment. The space before the front door resonated with the memory of the sports car; the living room, the TV, the seats were all redolent of the car owner.

'Sit down,' Alice said; she threw her bag into a seat. Lomba sat down.

She was not boasting when she said she had stacks of soul records. There were over thirty in the box she lugged out of her bedroom.

'They are all new!' he exclaimed.

'Well-preserved. My father bought them before I was born.'

He got down on his knees beside her and took out the LPs

one by one: Eddie Floyd, Funkadelic, Sam Cooke, Otis Redding, Marvin Gaye, Smokey Robinson, Percy Sledge, etc.

'Let's play them,' he said, but he could not see a turntable anywhere.

'The player is in the bedroom. I play them when I can't sleep. Let's go in.'

He must have shown his hesitation. She said, 'Don't worry, I am all alone, my flatmate has gone on a journey.'

He took the box and followed her. In the bedroom he put it on a settee against the wall. The carpeted floor was littered with female things — body-cream containers, perfume bottles, shoes — and a book or two. She bent down and attempted to clear the floor, then stopped halfway.

'Sorry about the mess, but I never planned to have anyone in here.' She cleared a place on the bed and told him to sit down. They agreed to play Percy Sledge first.

She kicked off her shoes and stretched out on her back beside him. He was seated on the edge of the bed, staring at her upturned face; her eyes were closed as she hummed along to 'When a Man Loves a Woman'.

'Do you think that is true?' she asked suddenly, opening her eyes, catching him staring intently at her face.

'What?'

'Do you believe a man in love is so naive? Does he really do all those things the song says?'

Suddenly his mind flashed to a vision of her in the mulatto's arms, the wet kiss. He shrugged. 'I wouldn't know. I guess most people in love might be like that.'

'No, I am talking about you.' She sounded curiously insistent; her eyes were steady on his.

'It has never happened to me.'

She got up on an elbow. 'You mean you've never been in love?'

He nodded, half-smiling. 'I've mostly admired, but not really loved.'

She gave a mock frown and opened her mouth, exaggerating her astonishment. 'Not really loved. How old are you?'

'A hundred this birthday.'

'Serious.'

'OK. Twenty-two.'

'Same here. But what have you been doing all this while?'

'Waiting for you, of course.'

She smiled and lay back. 'I am listening.'

He was joking at first, but as he talked he realized how convinced he was of his own words. 'I did not know I was waiting for you, of course, but the very first day I saw you I knew I had been waiting for you. Why? I don't know. But sometimes you meet someone and they are everything you've ever imagined and desired in a lover — from the way they speak to the colour of their skin to the way they walk and laugh. Anybody else apart from them would be imperfect. It is true.'

'And I was perfect for you?' she asked.

He felt bold, so sure of himself. He reached out and traced his hand over her face. She closed her eyes. Just then the record ended. She got up and went to change it. She glanced at her watch. 'How time flies! It is after eight already. You must be very hungry, and I am afraid I have no food in the house. Only Coke, or tea if you prefer.'

'I think I should be going.' Lomba said it without thinking, without meaning it.

Alice turned and faced him, the record in her hand. 'Why? Do you have something pressing to do in the hostel? You could spend the night and go early.' She spoke in a rush, as if scared that if she stopped halfway she wouldn't have the courage to complete her statement.

When she returned to the bed, he took her in his arms and kissed her. She sucked on his tongue. She laughed when they came up for air and said, 'I thought you were never going to do that.' He kissed her again. He had dreamt of this moment many times. Everything felt unreal, as if he was in a dream, or watching a film of himself, but in another life, another dimension. She hugged him tight, as if she also had waited and dreamt of this moment. They forgot hunger and Coke and time and the song from the player.

They kissed and made love. After, she grew talkative. Laughing at the tiniest hint of a joke in his statements. She asked him questions.

'What are you going to do after school?'

'I'll become a writer.'

'You mean a journalist?'

'No, a writer. Novels and poems. I'll dedicate my first book to you. "To Alice, the Love of My Life".'

'Promise?'

'Promise.'

What light and winged things promises are, fluttering away on the wind no sooner than they are uttered. I also promised to meet you the next day when I left you in the morning, a happy smile on your face. I had a happy smile too. I look back at my life, before and after that moment, and I daresay that that was

about the happiest moment of my life, that moment spent with
you. We were not to meet again for over three years — because
my friend went mad, because of the riots, because I dropped out
of school, because of so many things. What was a mere promise
in the face of all these cataclysms, what was love but luxury?
But life's paths are never straight, they wind and turn and con-
volute and return long-lost friends back together again — only
now when they meet things can never be like they used to be:
we have gone through so much sea change on our long voyage.
We have acquired other tendencies, other appetites, other loyal-
ties, and other pains. And other lovers: for me there was Sari-
mam — my other great love — but no two loves, or pains, or
loyalties can ever be the same.

LOMBA HAD GONE to the Mercy Hospital in Ikeja to capture the dying paroxysms of a once-famous high-life musician suffering from Aids for *The Dial*'s arts page. After the
slow and painful interview, he stood outside recovering,
removing the cassette from the recorder — and there she
was before him. He had seen the car come to a stop, he had
seen the pretty girl step out and wave to the man behind the
wheel; the car left and Alice stood there before him.

'Alice!' he exclaimed. He made no effort to conceal the
pleasure and surprise in his voice.

'Lomba!' In her voice too there was pleasure and surprise.
She was wearing a light-blue dress with black shoes; a broad
snakeskin belt hugged her waist, accentuating her curves. And
her face . . . How could he describe Alice's face other than to
say it was her face, unchanged, yet subdued, more mature.

'It's been long,' he said superfluously.

'Yes,' she replied.

He pointed to the food flask in her hand. 'You came to visit someone?'

'Yes, my mother.'

'Oh,' he said. 'She is ill?'

The mother had breast cancer. It had been discovered too late. The breast had been removed, but the rot had already infected other cells. She was dying.

She took him to see her mother, who had a room to herself. There were women, plenty of them, in the corridor and inside the room. Relations, friends, church members; they had come to be with her in her final moments. She looked so tiny in the narrow hospital bed, swaddled in the white hospital sheets, like a child. Her face was bony and drawn, yet when she opened her eyes a certain vitality still persisted in the sunken pupils — a death-defying light. He stood by the door, at the edge of the mat on which the women sat. They moved their legs, making room for Alice to reach the bed. The room was dark, close; a small, earthenware pot in a corner contained incense on coal, but beneath the smell of incense the odour of putrefying flesh was noticeable, a faint subterranean smell of death. Alice put down the food flask on a stand and sat on the edge of her mother's bed. She took the shrivelled, claw-like hands and whispered softly, 'Mother.'

'Alice. You are here.'

'Yes. How are you feeling?'

'Better. How are your brother and sister?' The voice was faint, whispery.

'Fine. Uncle Ngai will bring them after school.'

There was a pause, then the mother asked, 'And your father, has he phoned?'

Lomba noticed a tremor in the voice. Alice did not answer immediately; she leaned forward and flicked away an invisible speck on the sheets. 'He hasn't phoned.' She looked up, as if seeking a distraction. She waved Lomba over.

'Mother, this is Lomba. We were in school together.'

He went to the bed, bowed, feeling so inadequate, so out of place in this room full of women and the odour of death. 'Good day, Ma.'

She turned to him. From this close the smell was overpowering. Her face was atrophied, wasted. 'Hello, my son. Thank you for coming.' She sounded tired.

When she fell asleep, Alice took him for a walk.

'I am not keeping you, am I?' she asked. She sounded anxious, she did not want him to go. They took a path that led to a quiet clearing away from the wards. They sat on a log under a huge, shady nim tree. 'This is where I come to be alone.'

He was surprised when she brought out a packet of cigarettes and lit one. 'When did you start smoking?'

'Back in school, in final year. You were gone then. Why did you drop out?'

The memories came washing over him like waves. He shrugged. He felt sad all of a sudden. 'I guess I was exhausted.'

'And what have you been doing ever since?'

'I am a journalist. I am trying to be a writer.'

'Yes. You were going to be a writer. Are you published yet?'

'Not yet.'

They talked only of small things. She had graduated last year and was now doing her one-year Youth Service with a bank in Victoria Island. He wanted to ask her who the man in the car was, whether she was married, or engaged, if she still remembered their night together. He did not.

He took to coming to the hospital every day after work, and earlier on weekends. They did not talk much. Alice's face would light up visibly when she saw him. When her mother slept, they would retreat to the nim tree and smoke and listen to the crickets in the bush by the fence. Sometimes he'd bring her copies of *The Dial* and she would flip through the arts pages, making brief comments, asking questions. There was an air of waiting about their reunion, undefined, pendent, as if they were expecting a certain moment to arrive when everything would automatically fall into place.

One day she did something unexpected. They were seated side-by-side on the log when she suddenly reached out and took his hand in hers and pressed it to her chest.

He looked at her, surprised. 'What?'

'I am glad you reappeared when you did. Your coming gave me so much courage. I was so close to despair,' she said and released his hand. They sat and watched the shadows lengthen on the ground and the lights begin to appear in the wards.

Sometimes she'd leave him under the tree and hasten to the room where the shadows daily grew even thicker round her mother. Alone under the tree, he'd imagine her in the room, and the women who would be standing round singing and praying, the incense in the corner and the cloying smell of rotting flesh making a mockery of the incense. He would imagine the despair on her face as she felt closed in and trapped. He often compared her state to that of the messenger in Kafka's *Great Wall of China*: the Emperor, on his deathbed in his innermost chamber, has summoned the messenger and whispers a very important message in his ear, a message to be conveyed immediately to the remotest part of the empire. No one knows more than the messenger the absolute futility of his mission — first he has to get out of the innermost chamber with its thousands and thousands of courtiers impeding his progress, and after that there are a thousand outer chambers to traverse, still filled with courtiers; and though he is able to get out of these chambers (it will take him years), how can he manage to elbow his way past the millions of people waiting in the courtyard?

After the whispered message, Alice would turn and see the women watching her mournfully. In her agitated state she'd imagine their number multiplied a thousand times, hemming her in, and the smell would settle around her, pulling her down with strong, invisible hands. Above, her mother's spirit would be flying round, beating its wings against the ceiling, drawing closer and closer to the window every day.

On the last day Lomba went to the hospital, the women were not there. He looked at Alice in surprise. Only her mother lay on the bed, snoring lightly in the stifling evening heat. She read his questioning look and pointed out through the window. They were out under the trees, taking some air. There were only himself and the mother and Alice in the room.

'Alice,' the mother whispered. In the two weeks since he first saw Alice outside the hospital, Lomba had watched her mother grow weaker and weaker, smaller and smaller, till she looked like a baby doll in the narrow hospital bed.

Alice went forward to the bed and sat on the edge. 'Mother, you are awake.'

'But not for long, I am afraid,' the mother whispered. 'Come closer, you too.'

Lomba moved closer. In the corner the incense burned furiously, as if trying its best to ward off the death that hovered determinedly in the air.

'Alice . . . soon I'll be gone . . .'

'No Mum, don't say that. The doctor . . .'

'Forget the doctor. What does he know about death . . . ?' her voice trailed off. She closed her eyes, as if to sleep, then she opened them again; this time they seemed to glow with hidden vitality. When she spoke her voice was stronger, determined, like an old actor's on his valedictory appearance. She reached out a tiny, bony hand and took her daughter's hand. She fixed Lomba with her eyes. When she spoke, there was deep melancholy in her voice: 'You are so young . . . and this world is full of falsehood . . . Before you know it, it is all gone, youth, laughter, all . . .' Her voice wavered, like a flame in the wind. 'I am glad you two are in love. Don't play . . .'

'Mother!' Alice cut in, turning a half-amused, half-embarrassed look at Lomba. He avoided her look. Exhausted, the mother slept.

Outside, by themselves on the log beneath the nim tree, Alice began, 'I am worried about Mother. This illness is affecting her mind. See what she said about us.' She gave a laugh and shook her head. When he did not reply, she went on, 'You were not embarrassed, were you?'

'No, why should I be? I love you.'

She said nothing further. They sat in silence. Night was closing in, easing out the twilight that seemed to have lasted so inordinately. He took her hand. She sighed and squeezed his hand. She made as if to speak, but she only sighed once more. Her mind seemed to be heavy and far away. He watched her statuesque profile against the dying light: the long, uptilted nose, the full lips now slightly compressed, the hair, the chin, the cheek.

She turned and looked at him. 'There is something I ought to tell you, something I think you should know.'

She sounded so serious; he felt cold all of a sudden. 'Tell me.'

'Today Ngai asked me to marry him.'

Ngai. He had heard her mention the name before. The man who always brought her to the hospital in the big car. He recalled the greying hair, the snub nose, and the eyes that seemed so sure of their authority, eyes that would never quit short of the set goal.

'I was going to ask you the same thing.'

Her eyes bored into his. She shook her head. 'Oh Lomba, be serious.'

'But I am perfectly serious. Look at me, Alice. I've always loved you, even after I left school. I never stopped loving you. Do you remember what I told you that night in your room, when I spent the night in your room? I told you you were my ideal person. I think of that night whenever I hear Percy Sledge playing. Don't you remember that night whenever you play that song?'

'It was a long time ago, Lomba. Besides, I don't play those records any more, I gave them all away.'

Suddenly Lomba felt deflated, as if this one admission had foreclosed any chance of his ever regaining her love. His one trump card had been thrown back in his face. *She did not listen to soul music any more.*

He went on, but only as a drowning man flailing about, clutching at straws. 'Since that night, no single day ever passed without something bringing you to my mind. All my poems are dedicated to you. And when I saw you again I felt it was providence bringing back to me the only thing that had ever made me happy, I . . .'

'Stop, Lomba, stop, please.' Her look was anguished; her hands were raised, as if to ward off the dart points of his words.

He stood up and paced the small space in front of the log. 'Why should I stop? I have waited so long to say all these things; I might as well say them now, because after today it may be too late. I have waited, Alice, so long.'

'But you don't understand. What you are asking is not possible.'

'Not possible? Why? Because he loves you more than me? Because he has more money? Why? Give me one reason, Alice, just one.' He saw the stricken look on her face and realized that he had gone too far. He returned to his seat. 'I am sorry. I did not mean that.'

When she spoke her voice was impersonal, distant. 'Don't be. It is true. It is the money. Are you shocked? Do you know how much it costs to keep my mother here a day? Twenty thousand naira. This is the best cancer hospital in the country. Twenty thousand, and she has been here over a month now. Where did you think the money came from — my father? My father has left us. Over one year now. He is in Abuja with his new wife. Ngai pays for everything — everything, including this dress I am wearing. Now do you understand?'

He did not answer. He only stared into the night dumbly. He felt her hand brush his, and her voice whisper, 'Lomba, I am so sorry. So sorry. You must hate me now. Do you?'

Hate you, Alice, how could I? You were the idol of my idolatry. And even now, two years later, in my prison cell, as I look at the picture of you beside Ngai, in your wedding gown, all I can think of is the feel of your lips on mine when you kissed me that night before leaving me on the log under the nim tree. Later, much later, after your confession, I had asked you, 'Don't you feel something for me, even a little?' I was looking for a keepsake, a souvenir to bring out and caress later. It was as if I knew I would one day end up a prisoner, forever separated from you. You did not answer me. You stood up and started to go, then you turned back and took my face in your hands and planted a feverish kiss on my lips. You turned and ran off towards the lights in the wards. I wonder why he waited so long before marrying you — was it to give you time to recover after your mother's death? Or could it be that you were hoping, hedging, praying that I would . . .

'YOU NO DE tire, you don look that picture for hours now, abi you know dem?' a voice in the gloom muttered, shaking

Lomba out of his reverie. It was one of the inmates; it was he who had brought the paper. The paper was months old, but it did not matter. It would go from hand to hand, eagerly read by anyone who could read, till it was tattered and undecipherable. The man reached for the paper; Lomba released it reluctantly. How was he even sure it was Alice? It could be mere resemblance; but what of Ngai . . .

'Fine girl, abi?' the man whispered, admiring the picture.

Lomba nodded and whispered softly, 'Yes, very fine.'

LOMBA

WHEN I LOOKED out of my window and saw the youths crossing the bridge towards the rising sun, I decided to go out and get a life.

There were six of them, three boys and three girls, walking in pairs, in a procession. Watching them, I felt curiously breathless; their beauty was astonishing. The sun was shining straight into their faces, accentuating the comeliness of their features. They were like those rare, multicoloured birds one sees in the zoo; their laughter was birdsong.

I wanted to call out to them and invite them to my room,

but when I looked round the room a deep despair overcame me: unwashed dishes in the corner; unmade, book-covered bed; papers and pens strewn all over the table; and above it all the reading lamp throwing a weak, ghostly light.

Now they were almost at the end of the creaky iron bridge that straddled the huge gully that ran beside my compound. Ah, I thought, that I were one of them, out in the sun with a girl and so free. Perhaps I should return to bed, take an overdose of Valium and sleep. Let the world go on without you. Nobody would miss you — they never really do, do they? A day passes and a neighbour peeps in and says, 'Hey, you were not out yesterday.' Another day, and another day, and the enquiries stop. You are forgotten in the stymied, sense-dulling miasma of existence. And you lie there dead, or simply hibernating. It is as if you never really were.

I decided to get a life. 'I am only twenty-five, for God's sake!' I said to myself.

For the past two years I had been locked in this room, in this tenement house, trying to write a novel. For my bread I taught English and literature an hour daily, minus Sundays, in a School Cert. preparatory class run by a woman who always looked at me suspiciously, as if wondering what I did for a living. I looked at the papers spilling out of a thick folder on my table. The words and sentences, joined end to end, looked ominously like chains, binding me forever to this table. I felt a deep, almost fanatical loathing for them. Two years, and still no single sentence made sense to me. Standing by the window, staring at the manuscript, I felt, with epiphanic clarity, that if I sat down and picked up my pen and added a sentence more to this jumbled mass, I'd die.

The uncompleted novel would grow hands of iron and strangle me to death.

Without brushing my teeth, without washing my face or combing my hair, I slipped on my shoes and got out, my manuscript in a folder under my arm. I took a bus to Allen Avenue. I was going to James Fiki, *The Dial*'s editor. Two years ago (how time flies!), he had promised me a job. That had been my first and only time of seeing him. He had met me in my lecturer's office, submitting an essay titled 'The Military in Nigerian Politics'. He had sat in a corner, listening to me elaborate on my essay.

'OK, OK. I am convinced,' Dr Kareem said finally. He passed the script to the visitor. 'Here, James, take a look. See what university education has come to.'

The man read it quickly, then he returned it to Dr Kareem. When I was leaving, he said to me, 'Come and write for us when you graduate.' He gave me his card. The next week my essay appeared in *The Dial*, unaltered.

Well, I had not graduated, but I needed a job. As I climbed the stairs to the editor's office, I prayed that James would remember me, that he'd still be inclined to give me a job — if he still worked for *The Dial*.

He recognized me.

'Dr Kareem told me you dropped out of school,' he said when I sat down. He looked drastically older than he had looked two years ago. He couldn't be above fifty, but his hair had gone totally white; his suit was rumpled, as if he had not changed it in days. But his eyes, though red and puffy, were still sharp and secretly amused, as if he knew something you didn't know about yourself.

'Yes,' I replied. He waited, but I did not volunteer more information.

'And what have you been doing since then?'

I put the folder before him. 'I've been trying to write a novel.'

'That's why you left school?'

I did not tell him about the riots, about the incessant closure of the schools, or about my room-mate who went mad.

'When school began to look like prison, I had to get out,' I said simply.

He nodded. His eyes ran over my worn-out shoes, my threadbare shirt and trousers, my uncombed hair, my pinched, hungry face. He went through the manuscript quickly. He seemed unsatisfied. He said, 'What I need are articles and reports, not a novel. What you need is a publisher, not a magazine.'

'I need a job.'

He closed the folder. He said, 'You write so well, you express yourself so effortlessly, with so much force. I think you will do justice to almost any subject you care to write on. Tell me, have you ever thought of writing on politics? I remember your article on the military regime that I published.'

I shook my head doubtfully. 'I am not very political.'

'You can't escape it. In this country the very air we breathe is politics.'

He stood up. His tall frame had a stoop to the shoulders, as if he carried some unseen burden. He went to the window and pushed aside the thick blinds. 'Come here.'

I went and stood beside him. We were on the top floor. He pointed to the street below.

'Look out there, see the long queue of cars waiting for fuel. Some of them have been there for days.' He turned to me, the amused look now pronounced on his handsome face. 'And we are a major producer of oil.'

We returned to our seats.

'This is just one instance. If you care to look, you'll find more: ethnicity, religion, poverty. One General goes, another one comes, but the people remain stuck in the same vicious groove. Nothing ever changes for them except the particular details of their wretchedness. They've lost all faith in the government's unending transition programmes. Write on that,' he finished abruptly.

'On what?'

He waved his large hands before him. 'The general disillusionment, the lethargy. You can be as imaginative as you want, but stick to the general facts.'

I nodded. 'I'll bring it tomorrow.' I didn't know exactly what I was going to write, but I would do it, tonight.

WHEN I RETURNED to the tenement house they were taking Nkem away. The police, there were five of them, were dragging him forcibly to their van parked before the compound. When he saw me alight from the bus he wrenched free of the policemen's restraining hands and rushed to me. His face was bloody, one eye was swollen and it kept blinking as it tried to focus on me. He took my hand; there was manic urgency to his every gesture.

'I'll be back. It is misunderstanding. Settlement matter, that is all. I will be back.'

They dragged him away. Even as they forced his head into the van he tried to turn to me.

'It is misunderstanding matter, that is all.'

I passed the gawping neighbours and went into the dark corridor. My closest neighbour on the right was standing before her door, as always. She seemed to know my foot-steps, to know them from as far away as the compound entrance, because she'd always be standing here when I came in: before her open door, her shoulders bare, her wrap-per loosely held at her bosom, one breast half-exposed. Her eyes would brazenly stare me down, taunting, tormenting. Behind her was her bed, always slightly rumpled, as if she had just left it at the sound of my footsteps. She never said a word to me. When I entered my room I'd hear the sound of her door closing. Through the thin wall I'd hear her footsteps and snatches of raucous bar-room songs. She sold *ogogoro* and whiskey. Her loud and quarrelsome customers were a trial to me in the nights when I sat down to write. Sometimes a favoured customer would stay behind after the others had left, and deep in the night when I sat down to write, her exaggerated moans and the creaking of the bed beneath them were sore trials to me.

My compound was a block in a row of identical blocks, distinguished from each other by the faint black numbers on their front. I lived in No.15. When the sun was high, the roof crackled and spat. The buildings were long and tubular — from above they'd look like worms stretched out in the sun to dry. A long, cavernous passage led from the entrance to the door of each room; ten in all, five on either side, facing each other (face-me-I-face-you, the tenants called this formation). The toilet, an outhouse at the back, was open-air, and at night, squatting over the ass-scalding latrine pit, one could raise one's eyes and contemplate the sometimes cloudy, sometimes starry sky.

It was at the outhouse that I first saw Nkem, early one morning. I had gone to crap and had found the door locked from inside, but he was just finishing.

'I don't know you,' he said when he came out. His eyes were red and suspicious. He was huge and dark. His face looked sinister with its thick beard.

'I just moved in,' I said and passed him into the latrine. Inside was hazy with marijuana smoke.

I met him waiting for me in the corridor when I returned. He stepped forward, blocking my path. He thrust out a huge paw and smiled.

'I am Nkem. I am facing you,' he said, pointing at his door. He took to coming to my room in the mornings. He'd pick up my books and turn them over and over in his hands, painfully mouthing the words on the cover.

'One day I must return schooling.' His English was a tortu-ous parody of correct grammar whenever he spoke to me — but to everyone else in the compound he spoke pidgin. He seemed almost desperate in his efforts to impress me. He'd pick a page I had just finished writing and follow the scrawled, barely intelligible characters with his eyes.

'You write this?' he'd ask. 'Are you student?'

'No. I am a writer. I am trying to be, that is,' I said.

I didn't discover what he did for a living till my fifth month in the compound, till the morning he woke me up and pushed a carton of corned beef into my room.

'Eat,' he said, 'my friend give me dash.'

And before I could say anything he was gone. I stood looking at the carton, unsure what to do with it. Then in the evening, when I returned from my teaching job, my neighbour said to me, so softly I didn't hear her at first till she repeated herself, 'Your friend na thief o, softly de follow am o.'

I looked at the tormenting breast, the taunting, worldly wise eyes, and behind her the rumpled, still-warm bed.

'I see,' I said.

I saw it all: the footsteps trafficking the corridor late at night when I sat writing, or when I paced the room with insomnia; the early-morning returns. I remembered a glimpse I once had of his room; it was stacked with all sorts of stuff — TVs, fridges, tape players, chairs, and piles of clothes carelessly thrown into the chairs — like an emir's chamber, like a bargain store.

That night, when he came to my room, I told him to take away the corned beef. 'I am trying to become a vegetarian.'

He was seated on the edge of my bed. I was in the chair by the window. His bulbous red eyes wavered off mine; they went quickly to his thick, mud-covered boots and the small bag lying by his side. He had just returned.

'Not all you hear can be true,' he said, still not meeting my eyes. 'Rumour-monging and gossipers full our compound.' Then, as if a thought had just occurred to him, he stood up and with an 'I'll be show you' he went out and returned with a snapshot in his hand. He dropped it on the table before me. It was a young girl. She had one arm around the smiling, bearded Nkem. She couldn't be older than fifteen. Her eyes were smiling happily and innocently into the camera. 'My propose,' he told me, smiling broadly. 'You see, I be responsible person. Soon I'll be marry her and she'll be come to live here. Then you believe. But forget rumour.'

ALTHOUGH JAMES HAD been too polite to say that the assignment was an induction test to see if I was good enough for *The Dial*, I approached the task in that light. The next day, when I brought the handwritten pages to him, he read them, then he leaned back in his seat and contemplated my anxious face.

'Good,' he said.

I sighed. I had spent the whole night writing and rewriting.

I use my street, Morgan Street, as a paradigmatic locale, the fuel scarcity as the main theme. The long lines of cars waiting for fuel at petrol stations and obstructing traffic I use as a thread to weave together the various aspects of the article; in front of the petrol pumps I place the ubiquitous gun- and whip-toting soldiers, collecting money from drivers to expedite their progress towards the pumps. I place the pot-bellied, glaucomatous kids of Morgan Street, with their high-defined ribs, beside the open gutters where they usually play; in the gutters I place a carcass or two of mongrel dogs worried by vultures. In shady corners, under verandahs and broken trucks, I position winos to pass the day in vinous slumber. For local colour, I bring in the aged and the dying to peep through open windows into the street at youths holding roach communions at alley-mouths — passing the stick from hand to hand, with knives and guns in their pockets, biding their time. To conclude, I use the kerosene-starved house-wives of Morgan Street. I make them rampage the streets, tearing down wooden signboards and billboards and hauling them away to their kitchens to use as firewood.

James didn't like the conclusion. 'Are you not laying it on a bit too thick here? Perhaps we should leave that part out.'

I nodded, concealing my disappointment.

I was assigned to the arts page.

'Today is Thursday — you come on Monday and start work. Remember, once in a while you will be required to cover political issues. Everything is politics in this country, don't forget that.'

GOING BACK HOME in the slow-moving traffic, I closed my eyes and contemplated my future, but after a while I sighed and placed everything in God's hands. What mattered right now was staying alive. That was what James said to me as I left his office: 'Some day you'll finish that novel. What matters right now is life. Remember, life is short, but art is very long.'

My eyes snapped open as the rickety Molue bus came to a sudden stop in the middle of the road. I leaned out of the window with the other passengers to see what was causing the block. There was a loud, angry murmur of voices in front. Women's voices. The women appeared, crossing the road. Housewives in a large body, some with infants strapped to their backs. They were all carrying hoes and axes and machetes.

'Na demonstration?' the elderly passenger beside me asked.

The sharp claw of déjà vu gripped me as I watched the women come to a halt before a huge wooden billboard. They set to hacking and sawing, pushing and pulling at it, and soon the billboard was on the ground; the sensual face of the man holding a pack of condoms bit the dust.

'Dis women de craze?' my co-passenger asked as we watched the women breaking up the wood and sharing it into small bundles.

'They are not crazy. They are just gathering firewood,' I explained to him. It was my writing acting itself out. And James thought I had laid it on too thick. I wished he were here to see reality mocking his words.

'I no understand,' the old man said.

I also don't, I wanted to say, there is so much we can't understand because we are only characters in a story and our horizon is so narrow and so dark.

WHEN I RETURNED to the tenement house, she was there by the door. I almost passed her like I always did, but her voice stopped me. 'You no go come inside?'

I looked at her wise, wise eyes, then I went in. I sat down on the rumpled bed. The warmth in the bed rose up like welcoming arms and hugged me.

KELA

AT FIRST I thought it was the heat that made them dream
on Poverty Street. But Joshua told me that people could
be dreamers even in cold weather. 'Kela,' he said, 'people
become dreamers when they are not satisfied with their reality, and sometimes they don't know what is real until they
begin to dream.'

The mornings were usually cool, but by eleven a.m. the
sun was already high in the sky, and by noon the heat would
really begin to show its hand: it would force the people off
the main street and back roads, and since the heat was worse
indoors, the people would sit out on their verandahs on old
folding chairs; they would throw open the shop doors and sit

before the counters, stripped down to their shorts and wrappers, their bare torsos gleaming with sweat. Gasping for breath, they would stare through glazed eyes at the long, tarred road that dissected the street in two. By two o'clock, the tar would start melting, making tearing noises beneath car tyres, holding grimly on to shoe soles.

And there were no trees on Poverty Street. The heat would comb the defenceless street unchecked (like the policemen that came after the demonstration), tearing into doors and windows, advancing from room to room, systematically seeking out and strangling to death the last traces of cool air hiding beneath chairs and behind cabinets, wringing out moisture from the anaemic plants that drooped in old plastic paint containers on window ledges. Dogs would bolt out of the doorways, their brains cooked senseless, their tongues lolling out of their mouths like pink sausages, to be run over by cars. The chickens simply folded their heads beneath their wings and died. By five o'clock, the heat, having established its mastery, would begin to lift. The dazed, prostrate street would totter to its feet, shake the dust and sweat from its pelt, and resume life where it had stopped.

Poverty Street's real name was Morgan Street, one of the many decrepit, disease-ridden quarters that dotted the city of Lagos like ringworm on a beggar's body. My Auntie Rachael's restaurant, Godwill Food Centre, was at No. 20, Poverty Street (or Morgan Street — this story in a way is about how the street came to be called Poverty Street, and about the people I met in my one-year stay there, people like Joshua, Brother, Nancy, Auntie Rachael, Lomba, Hagar, and all the others who through their words and deeds touched my life and changed it irreversibly). The street consisted of a single tarred road that ran through its centre — Egunje Road — and a tributary of narrow, dirt roads that led off Egunje Road to the dark interior of the street.

My auntie's restaurant was on Egunje Road. At the head of the road, like a showpiece, was the Women Centre. It was the biggest and newest building on the street. I didn't know what the women did there. I always passed them sitting out on the balcony on plastic chairs, eating and talking loudly in Yoruba. Everybody started using the shorter name, Women Centre, when the full name changed from Mariam Babangida Women Centre to Mariam Abacha Women Centre. The first name was still faintly visible, in white ink, beneath the hastily painted new name in blue. Behind the Women Centre was Olokun Road, the shabbiest and poorest of all the quarters on Poverty Street. Olokun Road terminated in the less squalid, but more notorious University Road. The latter was the flux point for all vices on the street: there were hotels for sex and alcohol, and there were doorways and alley-mouths for marijuana and cocaine. The sex workers were mostly young university girls from the neighbouring campus, hustling on the side to make ends meet. The street had one primary school, Morgan Primary School, and a secondary school, Morgan Comprehensive Day Secondary School, both state owned. They were situated side by side on, naturally, School Road. The church was on Church Road and the mosque on Mosque Road.

1

Joshua taught English and literature at the secondary school
a block away from his house. A room, really. It stood alone,
surrounded by blocks of unplastered, unpainted storey buildings occupied by noisy working families that hung their
washing — underwear, bed sheets, babies' nappies — on the
railings before their rooms, and threw their dirty water into
the road. A housewife would stand with the empty pail in her
hand and absently watch the water break into a million dirty
brown crystals before it hit the ground. The storey buildings
looked shaky, adventitious, as if the first strong wind that
passed this way would uproot them. The fronts and backs of
the buildings were hidden by huge hills of refuse that over-
flowed and constricted the path to Joshua's room.

A half-completed wall circled the room. The room was
squat and rectangular, its walls covered with distemper that
stuck to the hands. He was alone. The room blazed like a
lighthouse. The door and windows were open, the curtains
lifted — a trap for the passing breeze. He was seated at the
reading table by the window, staring out into the dark. He did
not turn when I stopped at the door and knocked.

'Come in!' he shouted.

I entered. 'Good evening, sir,' I said.

Still he did not turn. I began to feel uncomfortable, standing there within the door, waiting. Then he started and
turned. He looked surprised to see me. I was surprised that
he was so young. My auntie said he was the only person that
knew anything about anything on Poverty Street. This man

couldn't be more than twenty-five. (He was actually twenty-eight, I found out later.)

'Welcome. We've never met before . . .' he began, then he stopped and snapped his fingers. 'You are . . . you are Madam Godwill's nephew, from Jos?'

Everyone called her that, because of her restaurant. Her name was Rachael, Auntie Rachael.

'She said she'd send you over. Come in and sit down. What is your name?'

He was seated on the only seat in the room. There was only the bed left. He pointed at it. It was unmade and covered with clothes; I pushed aside the shirts and trousers and sat down. Now I had to turn my head to see him. He was back staring out through the window at the lighted windows of the storey buildings. His head was bushy; he had a goatee that made his pointed jaw more pointed, like a needle, and infinitely long. I told him my name.

'My name is Joshua,' he said.

Apart from the bed and chair and table, the only other furniture in the room was a big stack of books on the floor at the head of the bed, on the side near the wall. Perhaps he was an insomniac, like my father, whose stack of books lay in exactly the same position in his room. My father said certain books could act like sedatives when you can't sleep at night. I leaned over and picked up the one on top. The title was in a foreign language — not French. *Das Kapital*, by Karl Marx. But the text was in English. I leafed through it idly, waiting. I heard the chair creak; I closed the book.

'You like the book?' he asked, coming over. He was in jeans

and singlet. His feet were bare — the toes long, the big toes pointed away from the others.

'The title is not in English.'

'German. Karl Marx was the founder of Marxism — that is, if you consider Marxism purely as an ideology.'

I didn't understand exactly what he meant, but I nodded.

'He was a German Jew, he died in Britain. How come you failed your exams? You look intelligent.' He was standing before the door, facing me, twisting and untwisting his goatee. I was five eight, and he looked to be about the same height as me; but I was only fifteen. I opened and closed the book. I remained silent. Now he bent down so that his face was level with mine. He had bushy eyebrows: continuous and unbroken over the nose ridge. His eyes were huge and effulgent in his long, narrow face. They looked kind as he smiled at me.

'I'll help you prepare for your English and literature, that is what your aunt is paying me for — but I want you to know that I cannot make you pass. Only you can do that for yourself. It depends on how much you want it — in fact, you can achieve almost anything you want to in this world if you want it bad enough. Do you agree?'

I came to find out that that was his characteristic way of ending his statements, interrogatively, making you feel you were part of the decision; and often his suggestions were not too hard to agree with. I nodded.

'Good,' he said. He went and drew out his shoes from under the table. 'I have to go out now. Tell your aunt we've met. Tell her we'll start lessons next week, same time. OK?'

'OK,' I replied. He picked up a shirt from the jumble on

the bed and put it on. When I stood up, he said, 'You can stay if you want. You can lock up later. You can read or something. No? OK, I'll lend you a book. Not Marx. Take something else. Have you read *Treasure Island*?'

'Yes.'

'Good. Here's something on the author. Biography is about the best read you can ever have. It has a bit of everything inside it: history, psychology, literature, and also a lot of silly opinion. Read it — next week we'll start our lessons with a discussion on it. Is that OK?'

TWO DAYS LATER, on a Saturday, he dropped in at the restaurant and took me to the beach.

'Have you ever seen the ocean?' he asked when I brought him his plate of rice. I was helping Nancy, the cook and waitress, who had gone in to put her child to sleep. I had never seen the ocean — there were only rivers and lakes in Jos, where I was born and where I had lived all my life.

'Go and get ready. Tell your aunt I am taking you to the beach.'

At the beach he took me right to the edge of the water, past the confused mill of half-naked bodies throwing balls, riding horses bareback, arcing towards the weak sun on creaky Ferris wheels, or simply reclining in the sand that was so white and fine and plentiful. The sand grabbed at our bare feet as we walked, its gristly fingers inching up our legs below our rolled-up trousers. We sat by the water margin, our legs dipped in its frothy wash. In front of us the water was pale blue, but further in it was a deep indigo, stretching on and on until it disappeared in a white, smoky mist that hung like a curtain between heaven and earth. Its infinite vastness, its restless heaving and roar overwhelmed me. Joshua pointed straight at the misty horizon and said somewhere on the other side lay America. He said if the vast ocean were magically shrunk into a tiny brook, or a narrow river, we could be staring at some beach on the American coast — New York, perhaps. He said the world was not as big and incomprehensible as some people would have us believe. He said everything lay within our grasp, if only we cared to reach out boldly.

2

Brother's shop, covered by garbage heaps at the sides and at the back, also served as his house. It was made of corrugated iron, which leaked when it rained and cracked and expanded under the hot sun. In front of the shop was a burst pipe — deliberately axed — which shot out water all day. The jet, redirected by a funnelled zinc sheet, formed a pool in a hollowed-out space beneath the pipe. Women and children gathered there all day to wash piles of dirty clothes, fetch water, and gossip. This was done amidst much fighting and swearing.

Olokun Road was named after the mermaid that was said to come there sometimes in the night, transformed into a beautiful maiden, to wait by the roadside for her human lover. I often imagined her, standing perhaps in a recessed doorway, or in the shadows under a tree, hope and anguish etched on her pretty, delicate face as she waited in the pungent, alien environment in vain. The houses were old and craggy and lichened. The place had the unfinished, abandoned appearance of an underwaterscape. Crouching behind the bigger houses or in their own clusters were hastily built wood and zinc structures that housed incredibly large numbers of families: the fathers were mostly out-of-work drivers, labourers, fugitives convalescing between prison terms. Further in towards University Road were nightclubs and seedy room-for-an-hour lodgings, where girls in black miniskirts hung out in dark alley-mouths, smoking cigarettes and waiting for a car to slow down, for the window to roll down and the finger beckon.

From the open door of his shed, Brother looked out at the fighting women and the refuse heaps and the passing mongrel dogs and sighed, 'If to say I get money. If only I get money.'

The reclining, recumbent figures before him also sighed in solidarity. They smoked marijuana openly, passing the stick from hand to hand, blowing out smoke, stifling a cough. Brother took a deep drag and sighed again. He pushed the half-finished trousers he was working on into a bamboo basket and raised his good leg on to the cutting board.

'One day Allah go give me a million, I know it.'

'Amen,' his friends murmured, their voices languorous from marijuana. They were mostly drivers and park touts and mechanics back from work and reluctant to go home just yet. Brother, once a driver himself, spoke the same language as them and was their favourite tailor. They'd hang upon every word of his outlandish stories as, outside, the evening grew darker and the shapes of the ever-present women fetching water became blurred. Brother's words would hover above their faces in the dark, mingled with the smoke haze.

'To each of una, my friends, I go dash a thousand naira, no, ten thousand naira!'

'Ah, Brother. You be good man,' they murmured.

'No, twenty thousand! Who I get apart from una? I no get wife, I no get pikin. You be the only family I get.'

They nodded. Then they urged him on to their favourite part of the wishful narrative. It was obvious that Brother's dreams were as familiar to them as their own.

'Then I go throw send-off party. My send-off from life of poverty. I go repaint every house for this street. I go hire labourers to sweep everywhere till everything de shine like glass. All of us go wear *aso-ebi*, fine lace, and Italian shoes. The Military Governor and the Local Government Sole Administrator — all go come here. I go pay Teacher Joshua to write my speech for good colo English, no be dis kin' yeye English wey dem de teach children for school now. We go eat and dance and drink and smoke fine imported *igbo* from Jamaica, the type Bob Marley used to smoke. Then finally I go stand before the TV people dem for final last handshake with Poverty. "Oga Poverty," I go say, "we don finally reach end of road. We don dey together since I was born, but now time don come wey me and you must part. Bye bye. Good-night. *Ka chi foo. Oda ro. Sai gobe.*"'

'Haha!' the audience laughed in appreciation. Brother lit a lantern and in its sickly yellow glow he continued to ply his dreams. Sometimes the details of the send-off party were dwelled upon, the exact venue (usually the front of the shed — but cleared and cobbled and street-lighted — was chosen). Particular persons would be commissioned to see to particular aspects of the celebration — inviting the Governor, hiring the seats, buying the food and drink, and, of course, the trip to Jamaica to buy A-grade marijuana. The dream trip ate far into the night, till the chatter and passing footsteps outside grew quiet and the cold began to pierce with a knife and the hallucinatory fingers of marijuana slowly released their grasp upon their brains; then they got up one by one, stretched and yawned and mumbled good night, and disappeared into the dog-yodelling night to their wretched hovels.

OUTSIDE ON THE street, Brother was a hero. Women and children would point at him as he hobbled past on his one good leg and the wooden one and repeat to themselves the story of how he lost his leg to a soldier's bullet, two years ago, in the post–June 12 riots. By the time I was a month on Poverty Street, I had heard over five versions of it. In one version, Brother had killed two soldiers with his bare hands before a third soldier shot him in the leg (right, at the knee). This was the most heroic of all the versions. When I had asked Joshua if it was true, he had shrugged and said, 'You mustn't take everything you are told literally. Hyperbole is a legitimate device in storytelling. Most stories, in order to achieve maximum effect, have to be exaggerated.'

Another version I heard from Brother himself. It was on the day that I first saw him; it was also the day Nancy poured okro soup on his head. In the hot afternoons, business was always slow at the restaurant, and I could sit in the empty room with my dictionary to learn new words, or do exercises from past question papers. It was a Monday.

The restaurant was rectangular and long. The door that opened to the street had a bead curtain through which I could watch the cars pass whenever I raised my head — I was seated at the head of the long aisle, against the wall; immediately to my right was the door to the kitchen; before me, on either side of the aisle, were the tables covered with white-plastic tablecloths.

The sharp sound of Brother's peg leg on the floor made me look up. He was standing in the doorway, the bead curtain bunched in one hand, the other hand on the door frame. There were two men in the restaurant, eating. They looked up at the same time and said, 'Brother, Brother!' their mouths full of *eba*. Brother limped to the man nearest the door and shook his hand; he waved to the other. He was in a black kaftan, and even from afar I could see the beads of sweat on his tar-black face.

'This heat wan finish us *kpatakpata*,' he remarked, wiping his face with the back of his hand. He had a hoarse, smoke-scarred voice. He was a big man, and I could easily imagine him holding two soldiers by the neck, one in each hand, till they died. He sat down at the first man's table, in one of the white-plastic chairs with 'Godwill' written in dark paint on their backs. He lifted his head and caught me staring at him.

'Hey, boy! On this fan.' He pointed at the stationary fan above him.

'It is faulty,' I replied, staring curiously, trying to match the legend to the man.

He cursed and moved to another table. He carefully

stretched out his wooden leg beneath the table, clutching his thigh with both hands. His real leg stopped at the knee, where it was strapped into a leather receptacle at the top of the wooden part; his trouser-leg was folded to the knee, exposing the long, cylindrical wood.

'Come here,' he said, waving a hand at me.

I closed my book and went to him.

'I never see you before,' he said, running his eyes over me, as if I was an item on a shelf.

'Na Madam Godwill nephew,' the man by the door said before I could speak. Everyone seemed to know who I was. Strangers stopped me on the street as I passed to ask me about Jos; and I wasn't even a month in Lagos.

'Oh, the one wey de do lesson with Teacher Joshua,' Brother said, his face splitting into a smile. He extended his hand to me. His palm was callused, like a farmer's; his grip was firm. His stare was dull, his red eyes heavy-lidded, like a reptile's.

I nodded. He held on to my hand.

'So, how Jos be?' he asked, and before I could answer he went on, his eyes growing more animated as he progressed, 'I de go there every week before, the time when I de drive bus — Lagos to Jos, Jos to Lagos. Every week. How the weather for Jos? E still cold?'

I nodded. 'From November to March.'

'I sure say you don de miss the cold, eh? Here na so so heat full everywhere. Heat and soja. If the heat no kill you, soja go harass you.' He tapped his wooden leg. 'See this one, na soja gun do am. Six of dem, I handle five with my bare hands. When dem see say I go finish dem, na im dem carry gun shoot me for leg. You don hear the story, abi?'

I nodded.

'Tell me, wetin be your name?' he asked, at last releasing my hand. It was wet with sweat. I wiped it covertly against my trouser.

'Kela.'

'Good. Now go and tell that girl to bring me *eba* and okro. I am hungry.'

Nancy was back in the kitchen. I gave her Brother's order and stood watching her as she picked out a clean bowl, filled it with hot water and poured the garri into it to make the *eba*.

'A strange man,' I said, holding the pot cover for her.

'His real name is Mohammed. He is from the north, though he has lived here all his life. He claims he is related to your auntie, but it is all lies. Don't ever believe anything he tells you. That thing he smokes has turned his head,' Nancy said. She was in one of her bad moods; it could last for days. She dipped the spoon into the pot of okro soup. She cut viciously with her finger at the elastic trickle trailing the spoon like a tail. Nancy was short and dark; she had the quick, springy step of a tomboy. She wasn't pretty — her eyes were too small and close together, almost meeting over her nose; her mouth was too large — but when she laughed, her face became so pleasant that you forgot she wasn't pretty. But she didn't laugh often. She was always screaming and cursing at Mark, her three-year-old son. She was only twenty, five years older than I was.

When she took the food to Brother, she slapped the tray on the table, making the plates jump.

'Crazy girl,' he muttered.

The customers were used to Nancy's strange ways. Brother

washed his hands and began to eat. Halfway through the meal he stopped suddenly, his eyes bulging, fixed to the wall on his right. I stopped writing, waiting to offer assistance if he was choking. He wasn't. He was reading the graffiti on the wall; Nancy had made it this morning with her inexhaustible supply of coloured chalks. It was a hobby with her. The walls in our room were covered with graffiti. She could spend hours on it: cleaning, correcting, re-writing. All sorts of things: proverbs, clichés, epigrams, even couplets. The one immediately above her bed, in green chalk, read: *Today Here, Tomorrow Gone. Such is life*. Over mine she had written in red chalk: *Love is a Gamble*. She was a magpie for quotable lines — a phrase on a billboard, or on the tailboard of a truck, or in a magazine, would stick in her mind and she wouldn't rest until she had off-loaded it on some wall, mostly in our room. The one that seemed to be sticking in Brother's throat read: *Poor Man's Paradise* . . . I couldn't see his face clearly from where I sat, to determine if he was amused or impressed or annoyed. Slowly he turned and with oil-reddened fingers beckoned to me. I went.

'Who . . . who write this?' He wasn't amused. His eyes had grown redder. A bearded customer sitting across the aisle turned, surprised by his sharp tone.

'Take am easy, Brother. Na small boy.'

'Who . . . who write am?' The anger made him stutter.

I remained quiet, contemplating what to say, but luckily Nancy heard us from the kitchen and came.

'What's wrong with it? I wrote it,' she said belligerently. She stood beside me, her right hand on her hip, her foot tapping the floor.

'"Poor Man's Paradise",' Brother read out aloud. 'This one na insult to us, your customers.'

Nancy raised her head and looked at the graffito, as if seeing it for the first time. 'Insult? What do you mean?'

I could feel the charge from the tension gripping her every limb. Brother turned and looked at the other customers — there were five sweating, oily-fingered men in the room now, their hands suspended over their dishes, their expressions uncertain, expectant.

'Because we carry our hard-earned money come de chop for here, na'im you de call us poor, abi? Poor Man's Paradise! Na our fault say we poor?'

'Look, I don't have the time . . .'

'No! Sharrap!' Brother's voice whizzed through the air, like a sword stroke, cutting Nancy off. His face glistened with sweat; his red eyes rolled. 'No. No try deny am. You can't. You de laugh at me because I bravely sacrifice my leg for this country, and now I am poor because I no fit work with one leg. You laugh at my friends here because dem de live for old and broken houses, because dem no get brothers in the army to thief and send dem money . . .' He was shouting now, hitting the table with his fist as he spoke. 'But make I tell you something — you de laugh at the wrong people. Make you go laugh at all the big big Generals who de steal our country money every day de send am to foreign banks while their country de die of poverty and disease. Dem de drive long long motor cars with escort while I no even get two legs to walk on. I, a hero. I fight . . .'

'Oh, don't start again with your lies!' Nancy cut in. 'Who did you fight? All of you. I was there when the soldiers and police came. You all ran and hid inside your wives' water pots, blocking your ears to the sounds of the soldiers raping your wives.'

'What!'

'Yes!' Nancy screamed, clapping her hands in Brother's face. 'You . . . you illiterate. It is not my fault that you don't understand English. Go back to school, you hear?' she hissed and turned to go. But Brother's hand shot out and grabbed her wrist. She tried to wrench free, but his grip was like iron. I saw the wildness rise in Nancy's eyes. She raised her small fist to strike him, then changed her mind. She snatched up the plate of half-eaten soup before him and brought it down, upturned, on his head. The plate fell back on to the table before rolling down to the ground. 'Bastard!' she hissed and pulled away her hand.

Now there was total silence in the room; only the screech of the rusty ceiling-fan turning filled the air. Brother had an incredulous smile on his lips as he raised both hands and touched his head. The gooey, mucilaginous okro soup trickled in slow motion down his face — eyes, ears, nose, moustache, beard — before disappearing into his shirt collar. He made no effort to stop the slow progress. He did not utter a word, did not even look at Nancy, who stood beside me, glaring defiantly at him, her face pinched and unrepentant.

I broke the silence. 'Let me get you some water . . . and soap . . .'

'No!' he said, gesturing with his hand theatrically, not looking at anyone. With both hands he pulled his wooden leg out from under the table then, leaning heavily with one hand on the chair, he stood up. The other men slowly stood up too.

Brother pushed aside the chair and stood beside us in the aisle. Nancy turned quickly and faced him.

'No be her fault. This thing for no happen if to say I get money,' Brother said slowly, his voice low, almost a whisper. 'No be her fault. Na poverty cause am.'

Nobody said anything. The men turned away from his gaze. The oily red soup covered his head like a martyr's halo. He made for the door slowly, the dull sound of his wooden leg on the floor breaking the silence at rhythmic intervals.

Then he was out and gone. I stood at the door, watching through the bead curtain as he walked down the street, still dripping okro soup, his head bent. People stopped and stared after him as he passed. From that day I took to ducking whenever I saw him coming towards me on the street. I felt guilty, as if it was my hand that had upturned the dish over his head. I was haunted by the infinitely sad expression on his face just before he left the restaurant: the theme of sadness emblazoned on every inch of skin, every wrinkle, every hair on his face — it was so impossibly perfect it looked inhuman, like a tragic mask.

3

Auntie Rachael dreamt backwards, groping back to a time dissolved, to figures blurred in the astigmatic lens of history. But I only realized that after I discovered that she was a secret drinker; after that it became easy for me to crack the riddle of the name 'Godwill'. I was led to it by the empty bottles of whisky that kept turning up: peeping out of the garbage bin under the almond tree in the centre of the courtyard, or in Mark's hands as he played; and sometimes half-empty on the window-ledge in the kitchen.

When I asked Nancy where the bottles came from, I heard her stifle a laugh. I turned and faced her. In the dark I could make out her shape. Her bed was beneath the window that opened to the courtyard; a thin stream of light entered through a hole in the zinc, pointing its finger at Mark's head behind Nancy. The room was hot and stuffy; the sharp smell of pepper and ginger mingled in the air. Our room also served as a store for my auntie's precious condiments, and sacks of grain and garri.

'Ask your auntie,' Nancy whispered. There was still the stifled laughter underneath her words.

'Auntie Rachael?' I was surprised, but suddenly everything fell into place: Auntie Rachael's splitting headaches in the mornings; her spell of frenzied good humour in the evenings; the curious stagger which at times left me wondering if she was unwell.

My father's eldest sister a secret drinker! I remembered the awed tone with which my mother had spoken of Auntie Rachael when she finally accepted the fact that I was coming to spend a year with her in Lagos. She had told me how Auntie Rachael had run away with her sweetheart when she was only eighteen; he was a no-good layabout whom her father swore she'd never marry. To my mother, who had grown up under a tyrannical father, the thought of any girl defying her father, and for love, was pure heroism. Now the feet of my mother's heroine were dissolving in cheap whisky. I felt sad. They had left Jos in the night, on a train (real romantic flit by moonlight) to Enugu. That was in 1960. Nothing was heard of them again till thirteen years later, after the civil war. Auntie Rachael wrote from Lagos to say that she was fine, but that her husband had died at Nsukka, fighting the Biafrans. She made no effort to return home. My mother said that Auntie Rachael was the most strong-willed and independent person she had ever known — perhaps because Auntie Rachael refused to remarry, even though she had no child. When I was only four, my father brought the family to Lagos to see her — my censorious grandfather had died the year before. It was the year in which she started the restaurant, and my only memory of the visit was of the fried chicken that I almost choked myself on. And of her teeth, bright like pearls. Now the brightness was gone, and she didn't laugh much any more. When I had appeared in the restaurant doorway, my bag in my hand, it had taken her only one look to recognize me — after eleven years.

'Kela, isn't it? My brother's son?' she asked, taking my hand. She showed me off to the customers, remarking that I was her brother's spitting image, but definitely handsomer.

Later, in her room, I answered her eager questions about home.

'So much time has passed. I fear I'll die without ever seeing home again,' she sobbed.

'But Auntie, you can go any time. Daddy will be so happy to see you,' I said.

But she only sighed through her tears and patted me on the arm. 'It is not so easy, Kela. So much time has passed, and we've all changed.' Then, as if not to spoil this happy moment, she wiped her eyes and said, 'But I am glad to see you.'

Now, as I lay on my bed in the dark, ignoring Nancy's snig-

I looked around: the room was dim, the light came in with difficulty through the heavy curtain on the single window. Everything in the room looked antique and faded. The TV was an old black-and-white, resting on a cracked table close to the wall. Behind the TV hung thick cobwebs with spiders dangling acrobatically in them; cockroaches scurried beneath the seats and table into cracks in the walls. The seats, facing the TV and the bed, had old, faded antimacassars draped over their backs and arms. An old pendulum clock with stationary hands looked down from over the door like a beneficent but tired ancestor; beside it, flowing into the adjacent wall, was a row of black-and-white photographs in wooden frames. The only picture in colour was that of a heavily bearded white man, like a hippy, symbolizing Christ. The dust lay inches thick everywhere; only the table on which her dead husband's picture stood looked neat, the picture frame shiny with constant polish.

'She can sit for hours staring at that picture,' Nancy said. 'Sometimes I have to shake her before she knows I am in the room.'

Nothing in her room was new: the TV, the radiogram, the black-and-white pictures, all were older than me. Her room was a shrine to a happy past; she kept her memories inside her, pickled in alcohol. I kept the money.

'Keep it,' Auntie Rachael said. 'Spend it wisely or return it to your father when you go back. I don't want to hear about it any more.'

So I did not tell her, seven months later, just before the demonstration, when Nancy stole half of it and ran away to Port Harcourt.

gers, I recalled a slight, disturbing smell on my auntie's breath as we talked that day: faint, faraway, elusive, like a mosquito's buzz in the dark. She must've just finished taking her morning tipple as I arrived. I was on a chair before her. She was seated on the edge of the bed; one arm rested on her knee. Her tie-dye batik dress — wrapper, blouse and severely tied scarf — made her look so prim, so matronly. She was only two years older than my father. On a table facing the bed was a framed photograph of a handsome young man in uniform, a rifle slung over his left shoulder. Her late husband, I guessed immediately. He was smiling; his youth and vitality came through powerfully in the photograph. I was startled by the thought that my auntie — with the lines on her face, the turbid flecks in her eyes, the thick veins on the back of her hands — had once been young and pretty and vital. Yet even now, at unguarded moments, when she laughed, or when the evening light fell on her in a certain way, one could still see the vestiges of her lost beauty, how she must have looked the night she ran away with her lover to an uncertain future.

'What for?' she asked me when I brought out the money from my bag and handed it to her. It was a lot of money. Ten thousand.

'I have to resit my papers, I failed the first time. This is for the lessons, and the exam.' But still the money was embarrassingly too much.

'Keep it,' she snapped, thrusting it back at me. 'Does your father think I am starving? Does he think I am so poor I cannot pay my own nephew's exam fees? Look, look,' she waved her hands around vaguely, 'does this look like poverty to you?'

'Is my auntie poor?' I asked Nancy. She did not answer me immediately. The bed springs creaked as she turned on to her back. Mark stirred beside her and muttered 'Mummy' before subsiding back to sleep.

'She makes enough from the restaurant. More than enough, but she spends most of it on drink. She calls it "pure water",' Nancy said grudgingly, as if I was forcing the words out of her mouth. She was that way: she hated to dwell on anything that threw a bad light on my auntie. Nancy feared no one, respected no one; she was self-destructively belliger-ent. My auntie was the only person she deferred to and, in her own crazy way, loved. When she left, she did not steal a kobo from my auntie, even though she could have done so easily.

Auntie Rachael had rescued Nancy from a life on the streets the day her father threw her out when he discovered that she was pregnant. Auntie Rachael had taken her in, and for over three years now they had lived together. As Auntie Rachael withdrew more and more into herself, neglecting the restaurant, it was Nancy that kept things going — buying food from the market, cooking it, selling it, and hiring the required help. And she kept the books with meticulous hon-esty. Sometimes I found her competence a bit daunting. But in the nights, when we couldn't sleep and we lay listening to the goats foraging for food out in the yard, we'd trade secrets; she'd tell me her secret dreams and fears.

'Do you think maybe he'd really come for me?' she'd whis-pered to me on more than one occasion. Mark's father. They had been in secondary school together. In their senior year she had given in to his demand for sex because he was leaving. His father had been transferred to Port Harcourt. Just once. Her first time.

'Does he know about Mark?' I asked.

Sometimes we whispered till the early morning. It was hard to sleep in the heat.

'Of course. He wrote to me.'

'Just once?'

She did not answer.

'He said he'd come and take me away. When he starts working.' She always referred to him as 'My Man'.

I also fell into the habit of calling him 'Your Man'.

The easiest way to get her out of her moods was to begin, 'Imagine Your Man walking in now.' It always worked, no matter how foul her mood.

And I told her the real truth behind my coming to Lagos. In the faceless dark, it was so easy to bare all; it was like talking to oneself. For all you knew, your auditor might be asleep.

'My father caught me smoking marijuana in his car one morning. Like you, it was also my first time.'

She didn't gasp in surprise. Maybe she was asleep.

I had gone down to the garage in the morning to warm up the car as usual — one of my assigned duties since I finished school. The already rolled marijuana was in my pocket. A friend had given it to me the night before; he had urged me to try it, assuring me of its 'different high'. I had lingered over the decision. Now, in the morning, with the car idling beneath me and the whole day stretched before me like a wasteland, I didn't find it difficult to press the car cigarette lighter and put the glowing end to the tip of the joint in my mouth. It was a different kind of high from cigarette and beer. He was right.

Then things happened that I had not envisaged: like my father coming into the garage, his footsteps muffled by the sound of the car engine; like the smell lingering accusingly in the car even after I had swallowed everything: paper, grass, and ash; like my father refusing to believe that it was my first time. Later, arraigned before the full council of my family: my irate, table-banging father, my weeping mother, and my kid sister, Olive (clearly silhouetted behind the kitchen curtain, eavesdropping), I couldn't help feeling tickled by the whole fuss, by my new evil-child status. I had been so ignored since I had failed my School Cert. last year.

'I caught him smoking weed, in my car. Weed, at his age! He failed his exams, now he is smoking weed!' I wondered in a detached, clinical way why my father kept referring to it as 'weed'. It sounded so old-fashioned. My friend had over ten names for it, all so new, so creative.

'I've decided. I am sending him to Lagos. Let him see how real life is. He will resit his papers there. One year — I want him out of my sight for a year.'

I had always wanted to go to Lagos — to return. I had been there once, at four. It'd be nice to have my family out of my sight for a year.

'But Dan,' my mother wailed, 'they'll kill him there. They are rioting and killing people on the streets there. Especially northerners.'

Behind the curtain I saw my sister's ears wiggle at the name 'Lagos'. My mother went on, 'It is in the news — a bus was stopped by the anti-Abacha people and anyone who couldn't speak Yoruba was slaughtered in cold blood. Northerners are leaving the south . . .'

'He is going by plane,' my father conceded. I had never been in a plane before. 'Get ready, you are leaving in the morning,' my father declared and stamped out. My mother followed him, begging. I removed my shoe and aimed it at the shadow behind the curtain.

Now, as I turned and turned in my bed, between sleeping and waking, I wondered: did my father know about his sister's drink problem, and was that why he sent me to her, so that I could see the debilitating effect of vice up close and be shocked back to my senses? And why was he so sure I would be shocked back to my senses? It could work either way, such proximity to vice, couldn't it? In the morning at the airport he had said to me, 'Your problem is that you've been over-sheltered, over-protected. In Lagos you'll see what life is really like, then you'll know what it is really worth, I hope.'

'She wasn't always like this, you know,' Nancy's voice suddenly whispered. She wasn't asleep. 'An addict, I mean. When I met her she was cheerful and happy — and a man wanted to marry her.' I got up on my elbow; my ears wiggled like Olive's behind the curtain.

'Who?'

'Our landlord, Alhaji Sikiru.'

'Well, did she agree?'

'She hadn't made up her mind before he was killed.'

'Oh!'

'In the Abiola riots, two years ago. He was burnt inside his car at Ajegunle. They thought he was a northerner. It was after that that she took to drinking.'

I felt sad. My auntie, it seemed, wasn't very lucky with men. Two, and both lost in the same violent fashion. It is only now, five years later, that I am able to crack the riddle of 'Godwill'. It was a wish, a prayer which vacillated between a golden past and a dark, unhappy future: Godwill return my past with all its joys and promises; Godwill not. He will do whatever He feels like doing, which is mostly destruction of dreams and hopes. Godwill. It was a worldview, not a sign-painter's error.

4

Hagar was Joshua's secret obsession. I found out about her on a Saturday when we were walking down University Road, Joshua and I; it was my fifth month in Lagos. We had returned from the beach, my head was full of tumbling water and fine bleached sand and buried shells and America hidden behind a mist. I bumped into Joshua when he stopped suddenly.

'Come, there is someone I want to see here,' he said, pointing at a row of three shops in the front of a big building. One of the shops, the Health Is Wealth Patent Medicine Store, was closed; one sold spirits — Johnnie's Hot Drinks; the other was a hairdressing salon, the Clever Fingers Beauty Shop. Beside the salon, a huge door opened into a short corridor; over the door flapped a row of plastic banners bearing the names of beer brands: Rock Lager, Gulder, Guinness Stout. A huge wooden signboard before the warehouse-like building bore the words MAYFAIR HOTEL. Bottle crowns crunched beneath our shoes as we passed through the doorway — a raw cocktail of drums and guitar and horns blaring from giant speakers placed just within the door gripped us as we stood and surveyed the hotel's courtyard. About half of the tables were occupied by men and women, all drinking and smoking. I looked at Joshua to confirm whether we were really at the right place, everything looked so . . .

'There she is,' he said, looking across the courtyard at a girl seated by herself at a table against the far wall. She had also seen him. She smiled and waved as we made our way to her. They didn't talk much; they just sat and stared at each other. Finally Joshua introduced me.

She shook my hand. 'I am Hagar,' she said. 'Kela. Such a cute name, with a cute face too.' She was smoking. She coughed until tears came to her eyes.

'You should quit,' Joshua said, his eyes concerned.

'Yeah — "Smokers are liable to die young." But who wants to live for ever, anyway?' she replied. But she crushed out the cigarette.

I had never seen Joshua this way before: laughing, his eyes shining, and reaching across the table to take her hand. She caught me staring at her long, natural hair, her perfect eyes and nose. I lowered my eyes, embarrassed.

'Kela, tell me about Jos,' she said, but before I could speak she had changed the topic. 'You mean you've been in Lagos five months and Joshua had not brought you to see me?' There was a teasing note in her voice. I knew her words were directed at Joshua, not me.

'This is not a place for him,' Joshua said.

But Hagar went on as if he had not spoken. 'He doesn't like coming here. Tell me, Kela, is there anything wrong with this place?'

I shook my head without speaking. I turned and stared at the bar, a window in a wall with iron bars through which the barman passed out bottles of beer and collected money. The next time she caught me staring at her, I stood up and said I was leaving. 'My auntie will be wondering where I am,' I said.

'But you haven't finished your Coke,' she said. I picked up my half-finished drink and gulped it down. 'Come here.'

I pushed back my chair and went round to her. She stood up. She was taller than me in her high heels. She bent down and kissed me on the cheek. I felt the soft moistness and the warmth as her lips moved against my cheek. Outside, I held my cheek where she had kissed me and ran all the way home, strange emotions rioting in my heart.

THE NEXT TIME I went to him, Joshua began talking about Hagar as if two days had not passed since we had gone to see her at the Mayfair Hotel.

'She was my student, you know. That was the year I came here as a youth corper, fresh from the university.' I was at the table, facing him as he paced the tiny room, to and fro, to and fro. His eyes avoided mine, they stared at the wall, sometimes they looked outside through the window. She was nineteen then, a little older than the others. Seated at the front, staring at his face as he elaborated, a bit confused, a bit self-consciously, on simile and metaphor. I imagined him in the nights, in this room, tormented by her eyes, her smile, her full breasts under the school uniform, sleepless and hallucinating so that he saw that sweet countenance floating on the ceiling above him — like on a movie screen. 'Oh, I got her notes, love poems. But what could I do? I was a teacher and she a student, and the rules were clear . . .' he paused and laughed. 'I have always been old-fashioned, you know.'

Twirling his goatee, his eyes faraway, standing still. 'And I wanted to be retained after my service, jobs weren't so easy to come by, even then.' Then Hagar's father died. Her mother took her and her siblings away to her parents in Warri. 'But she kept on writing to me. She had written her JAMB exams. She was going to the university to read English and litera-ture, like me. She was a brilliant student. The best in her class. Well, she passed her exams and went to the university and . . .'

Things started falling apart when her mother remarried. The stepfather was a drunk, and he soon drank his way through the mother's little earnings from her petty trading. And pinching Hagar's bottom whenever her mother wasn't looking. One day the mother found them struggling in the kitchen — the drunk's handshake had gone way past the elbow; from bottom pinching he had moved upwards to her breasts, and Hagar had slapped him. The mother, blinded by love, had misunderstood.

'She threw Hagar out. She said Hagar was trying to snatch her man. With no means of support, Hagar dropped out of school. That was when her letters to me stopped. A year passed, then one day I saw her before the Mayfair Hotel.' He sat down, as if his legs had grown weak. 'A prostitute,' he said, his eyes staring directly at me. The words hung in the air, like an unpleasant apparition. Still staring at me, he went on, 'Life. As you grow older, you'll find life demanding you to make certain choices. Some people choose the easy roads, some the hard ones; but they all have their reasons. Never condemn a man or give up on him because of the road he has chosen — because sometimes it is actually the road that chose him. People can change. People do change . . .'

I remember the pleading, almost desperate note in his voice. As if he was begging me to understand and not think less of him because of whom he had chosen to love. I could smell the odour of tragedy in their affair. As young as I was then, I realized that the affair could not end any other way but in tragedy and pain. Perhaps that was what made my love for the two of them so fierce, so poignant.

I TOOK TO hanging around University Road, skulking in alley-mouths and by shop fronts, my eyes fixed on the entrance of the Mayfair Hotel. I was there in the late mornings when the girls came out to buy beans and bread from the passing bean-hawkers, and sometimes in the evenings when they congregated in the hairdressing salon. But it was hard to distinguish their faces from a distance, with their heads covered by the hair-dryers. She never seemed to come out at all. I was lovesick. I just wanted to see her, even from afar, preferably from afar — for what had I to say to her face to face? Then one day, almost a month after our first meeting, I met her. I had taken to going all the way to Johnnie's Hot Drinks to get my auntie her 'pure water'. I loitered by the door so long after making my purchase that the toothless old man behind the counter shouted at me to get lost. That was when Hagar came in. She was in a black miniskirt and a white sweater; her hair was rough, tied in a narrow red bandanna. I opened my mouth and called her name. She hadn't seen me. She stopped and turned; her eyes lit up in recognition.

'Kela.' She remembered my name. I smiled. I nodded. 'What are you doing here?' she asked, but before I could answer she went on, 'Wait for me. I want to buy some cigarettes.'

When she returned, she took my wrist. I was sure she could feel my blood pulsating madly beneath the skin. 'You are not in a hurry, are you?' she asked. We were at the hotel entrance now, under the signboard. The bottle crowns looked like shells scattered on a dirty beach. There were broken bottles and paper bags and a dry patch on the steps that looked like vomit.

'No,' I replied.

She led me down a passage, past girls seated on doorsteps painting their nails, dressed only in loose wrappers and bras, their overnight make-up streaking down their faces, their wiry hair peeping out from beneath their wigs. The smell from a nearby urinal, mingled with last night's cigarettes, hung in the shadows determinedly, like an unwanted visitor. The doors faced each other on either side of the passage. Hagar's was the last on the right. When we entered, she opened the wooden window and raised the thick black curtain. A patch of light entered and fell on the bare floor between the bed and the dressing table by the window. There was a big mirror on the dressing table, inclined against the wall, and rows of shoes underneath.

'Sit down somewhere,' she said breezily, pointing to the bed. 'Welcome, welcome.'

She pulled out the chair by the dressing table and turned it round. She sat facing me. She kicked off her pumps and lit a cigarette. She shook it in the air after the first deep drag. 'Bad habit,' she exhaled, the smoke screening her face momentarily. 'Joshua is always after me to quit. You don't smoke, do you?'

I thought of another kind of smoke, in another place. Recently, I'd found myself missing home. My parents, even nosy Olive. I shook my head.

'But you drink whisky?' She eyed the paper bag in my lap.

'Someone sent me.'

'Next time, tell them to come and get it themselves.'

'I can't.'

But her mind was already somewhere else. 'It is so hot.' She picked up a paper from the table and fanned herself. Then she dropped it. She put the cigarette in an ashtray and pulled off her sweater. Underneath was a white bra, fringed with lace. The white contrasted beautifully with the chocolate of her skin. 'Better,' she said, blowing air through pursed lips into her cleavage. At first I found it hard to keep my eyes off her bust, the hypnotizing angle between breast and breast, but it got easier as we talked.

'Have you seen Joshua today?' The cigarette was suspended, forgotten, as she waited for my answer.

'Yes. He came to eat lunch at my auntie's restaurant.'

'Did he say anything . . . I mean, was he all right? I have not seen him in two days,' she said, her eyes on the almost-finished cigarette. Her voice was dull.

'He was fine.'

I was there for almost thirty minutes — once she got on to the subject of Joshua, she couldn't stop. She wasn't really talking to me — it was as if she had been waiting for someone to talk to. Her talk was disjointed, like a cured deaf-mute testing her voice for the first time. She asked questions and never waited for the answers before veering off on to something else.

'I was his student, you know,' she said and got off her stool. She went to the wardrobe and returned with a carton. It was filled with books. 'He still thinks I am his student. He brings me a book each time he comes. Look.' She brought them out. 'Shakespeare, Dickens . . . You like him? Keep this then, *Oliver Twist*. It is my favourite. And poetry. Look, look.'

She returned to her seat, throwing the cigarette butt out of the window. Outside was Olokun Road: the wooden shacks and zinc lean-tos slumped against each other, dehydrated by the scorching heat.

'He said I should go back to school. That he'd pay. I said no.'

'But you could go back. He said you were the best in your class,' I said.

'Imagine me in a class,' she went on, her eyes over my head, a wry grin on her lips. 'I'd feel like their grandma. I feel so old . . . so out of time. You won't understand, you are how old . . . fifteen? For you time drags, for me it gallops.'

I interrupted her, raising my voice. 'But you are young!'

'Oh, I am not talking about physical age. I mean here,' she touched her temple. 'I feel as if I've lived a hundred years. I am too old for him.' She sounded unhappy, but she went on voicing her thoughts, forcing her mouth to open, the words to tumble out. 'What he needs is someone younger, someone untainted. They want him to go into politics when democracy returns, did he tell you that?'

She turned round and pulled out the desk drawer. She

took out a file and opened it. 'Come and see. Let me show you.' I went over and stood beside her. She smelt of cigarettes and perfume. The file was full of clippings from newspapers. She took them out one by one. Some were literary: book reviews, essays; there were also longer essays on social and political issues.

'He wrote them all. He is so into politics — you didn't know?' She sounded proud and sad all at once. Some of the essays carried his picture; he looked so young in them. The pictures had his name underneath them. Joshua Amusu. 'He said he'd write a book one day. He has so much to do, I'd only be a burden to him. He doesn't need me.'

'He loves you,' I said.

She closed the folder gently, thoughtfully. She touched me on the cheek. 'I love him too. But sometimes love isn't as important as we think.' She lit another cigarette. I watched her smoke in silence. There was a deep crack in the wall behind the dressing table and mirror, running parallel to the window and disappearing into the ceiling. When I told her I was going, she stood up. 'Let me walk you out. Oh, I've something to give you.' She opened the drawer again and rummaged inside, throwing out packets of condoms. 'You don't need them, do you?'

I looked down, embarrassed. 'Take them anyway. They might come in handy,' she said with a wicked laugh. She thrust a pack into my breast pocket before returning to the drawer. This time she came out with a bottle of whisky. She gave it to me with a satisfied smile. 'I know you don't drink. I also don't take whisky. Someone left it here. Take it. Give it to the person that sent you. Tell them from Hagar.'

She walked me to the courtyard, past the iron tables and chairs, dressed only in miniskirt and brassiere. I felt relieved when she stopped before we reached the hotel entrance. She seemed reluctant to let me go. She put one arm on my shoulder as we stood facing each other. I could feel the eyes of the barman on us behind his iron bars.

'Tell him it won't work. Tell him to forget me. I belong to the past. I am like an appendix: useless, vestigial, even potentially painful. Tell him that.'

'SHE SAID THAT?' he asked when I gave him Hagar's message that evening. We were in his room, about to start *Macbeth*. I had only two weeks to my exams.

'She said she is like an appendix, a vestigial,' I added.

'A vestige,' he corrected automatically, twisting and untwisting his beard.

'What is a vestige?'

'A trace, a leftover.'

'But she isn't. She is nice . . . and so beautiful,' I said.

Joshua looked at me; he looked surprised by the passion in my voice. He smiled and stood up. 'Thanks. I'll go and tell her that right away. What do you think?'

5

In the nights, sweating beneath the sheets but unable to throw them off because of the mosquitoes, I'd lie half-awake, listening to the sounds of the night: the faraway dogs baying at the full moon; the goats out in the courtyard butting their heads against the garbage bin, trying to get at the yam peelings inside; the owls eerily cooing in the almond tree. Some-times, in my drowsiness, I'd mumble a statement towards Nancy's bed before catching myself. She was gone. Her bed was empty now. Though I used to be irritated by them, I refused to clean the multi-coloured graffiti on the walls; I left them as mementoes of her. She had left quietly one morning last week; she must have planned it for long, without telling anyone.

'The stupid girl,' Auntie Rachael had muttered over and over as she paced the space before this bed; between the two beds. She had stopped and stared hard at me, seated on the bed, and asked, 'Are you sure she didn't tell you anything before she left?'

When I shook my head, she sat down and went on talking to herself. 'Maybe it's because of that little incident with Brother. Do you think so? She was so upset, wasn't she?'

After the soup incident she had called Nancy and berated her and asked her why she had done it. 'Maybe you want to drive away my customers. Is that it? Would that make you happy, you ungrateful wretch?' They were the harshest words I had ever heard pass my auntie's lips. And as if ashamed of them, she had hurriedly said to Nancy, 'Go, go, leave me alone. I am not feeling well.'

That night Nancy had not slept. She had stared at the ceiling without moving a muscle. She had not turned even when Mark cried and cried and finally fell asleep. But in the morning she was her normal graffiti-scribbling self. As if recording the lessons she had gained from the whole inci-dent, she wrote — in deep black: TO BE A MAN IS NOT A DAY'S WORK.

After waiting two days, we had decided that Nancy was not returning. Auntie Rachael had gone and informed Nancy's parents. They had a tailoring shop at the Community Market. Mr Dahunsi, seated behind his sewing machine, had sighed and shrugged. Mrs Dahunsi had not even looked up from the cutting board.

'That boy, that stupid boy that impregnated her has a hand in this,' Mr Dahunsi said at last, his fanatic's beard quivering.

'Did she talk a lot about him?' Auntie Rachael asked me. 'The poor girl, she could have told me . . . did she think I'd stop her from going to him? She could have asked me for some money, at least.'

Nancy's restaurant accounts had been found to be scrupulously honest to the last kobo. That, instead of cheering up my auntie, only made her more depressed. 'All alone, with a child, without a kobo. Foolish girl.'

I did not tell Auntie Rachael that half of the eight thousand remaining from the original ten thousand was missing from my bag. I discovered the absence a day after Nancy's flight. From that day I took to going around with all the money in my pocket. But I didn't mind. I pictured Nancy in Port Harcourt with the tattered letter from Her Man, with the street directions to his house. I pictured her seated by the roadside on a bench, with Mark in her lap, tired of searching and looking into every face that passed, hoping to see Her Man. No. This picture was too dismal. I didn't want Nancy ever to be in such a situation. So one of the passers-by would pause after passing, he'd look back. 'Nancy, is it you?' It was Her Man. She hadn't recognized him because he had grown a beard, and he was taller, and . . . The dogs howled me to sleep.

6

In the past month, the gatherings in Joshua's room had become more vocal. Before, it used to be an occasional father staying behind to have a 'learned' chat after obtaining advice from Joshua on the best secondary school to send his child to — preferably somewhere private and cheap. Or a retiree seeking advice on how best to pursue his reluctant gratuity. The gatherings became more vocal as they became more political. They became more political with the coming of Mao. His real name was Ojikutu, but since he had come back two months before from somewhere in the Niger Delta, where he had done his one-year compulsory youth service, he had announced to anyone who called him Ojikutu, 'The name is Mao. Or Chairman.'

I'd be on the bed, away from them, my back against the headboard, my legs tucked beneath me, my knees forming a table for whatever book I was studying. Mao always came with an entourage: sometimes two, sometimes three shadowy characters who wouldn't utter a single word throughout the discussions. He had a transistor radio, and he always arrived at seven-thirty, the time for the BBC's *Focus on Africa* programme. We'd listen in silence as the announcer's voice painted a grim picture of affairs in our country: arrests of pro-democracy activists by the military government, and sanctions placed on us by foreign countries. Then one day, in

November, after my exams, we heard about Ken Saro Wiwa's hanging. We huddled close to Mao, who was seated at the foot of the bed, facing Joshua on the chair at the table and the two shadows on the mat on the floor. NEPA had taken the light; in the dull glow of the candle flame the two shadows looked even more shadowy, indistinct, merging into each other and into the wall behind them.

'This country is in dire need of a revolution,' Mao exploded in the thick, enveloping silence that followed *Focus on Africa*. Sometimes I found it hard to follow his speech. His words were sometimes so strange that they seemed not to be English at all. And he spewed them out so fast in his high, reedy voice: comprador bourgeoisie; lumpen-proletariat, reactionaries, militariat. He hated the military more than Joshua did, more than Brother, more than Auntie Rachael. Perhaps they had done something terrible to him. 'We have to utterly destroy the status quo in order to start afresh. Rawlings did it in Ghana — even though he preferred to continue in the same neo-colonial, capitalist mode.'

'How are you going to do it?'

'Start an uprising, of course, no matter how small. Things are so tense now that a slight spark will set the whole place ablaze,' Mao said, and his two shadows nodded. Mao was a huge man, with a thick beard and a balding dome. He looked like Emeka Ojukwu, the former Biafran leader. He growled as he spoke, pinning down his listener with his eyes. There was something comical in his exaggerated militantism. And sometimes I'd catch Joshua trying to suppress an amused smile as he nodded gravely at Mao's fist-waving comments.

'Look, we are living under siege. Their very presence on

our streets and in the government houses instead of the barracks where they belong is an act of aggression. They hold us cowed with guns so that they'll steal our money. This is capitalism at its most militant and aggressive. They don't have to produce any superior good to establish monopoly. They do it by holding guns to our heads. Let me tell you why they hanged Saro Wiwa. He was the only one who understood the economic aspect of the struggle. It is the money. He told Abacha, I know how much you and the foreigners are making — the billions you are drilling out of our soil. Give us some of it. They killed him because he threatened their monopoly, got it? Monopoly. That's what this is all about. Where is Abiola? In prison! They'll continue subjugating us, killing all dissenters, one by one, sending them into exile, till there is no competitor left to oppose them.'

'It is true. I agree,' one of the shadows said boldly and passed his cigarette to the other.

'According to Frantz Fanon, violence can only be overcome by greater violence,' Mao said. This time he turned to me as if for confirmation. I quickly lowered my head into my book.

'Can you?' I heard Joshua ask softly.

Mao put down the transistor radio and stood up, then sat down again. 'Don't underestimate the readiness of our allies to help us. They are waiting. They are eager. And with this thing that happened tonight, they'd be willing more than ever to help us — guns, weapons. All we need.'

And soon everyone on the street was talking about 'the revolution'.

'Soon, soon,' they would whisper as the army jeeps passed

our narrow roads. Although Mao was the drummer, it was Joshua's name on everyone's lips. Everyone seemed to be waiting for him to name the day.

'Are you going to lead the revolution?' I asked him one day. We were at the beach. He was standing on the mobile water line, his legs covered with sand and froth. His arms were folded over his chest; he was gazing absently into the horizon. At America, I thought. He sighed and rejoined me where I was seated on a little sand hill, safe from the waves. Nowadays he seemed distant, quieter. I liked to think it was Hagar he was thinking of. I wondered why he had never brought her along to the beach — or maybe they came together at other times. For, really, what did I know about him, about his real life, apart from the fact that he was my teacher, that he was in an impossible love affair, that he was going to write a book, and that for some reason everyone on the street seemed to look up to him, even Mao with his self-important posturing? He sat down beside me and picked up a shell and held it up to the sun, admiring its pale-pink colour.

'In a normal country there wouldn't be a need for revolutions; there wouldn't be a Poverty Street; well, not like ours, anyway. People like me would be able to teach in peace, live in peace and . . .' he turned to me and smiled, 'and maybe fall in love and marry and have kids and die old.'

He went on, 'That romantic fool. He has read too many books about revolutions in China and Russia. Now he thinks he can start one here with petrol bombs and maybe a couple of guns and knives. He'll get us all killed. He doesn't know what desperate people he is up against. Now everyone on the street is waiting for me to start a revolution.' He looked into the horizon silently for a long time. Then he sighed. 'Maybe I should just go away. Quietly.'

'What'll happen to Hagar?' I asked before I could stop myself. For the first time I saw something close to anger in his eyes.

'What about Hagar? She is not joined to me at the spine, is she?' He picked up a stone and threw it into the water with all his might.

ONE HOT, SUNNY afternoon, my auntie called Joshua into the kitchen when he came to eat. Since Nancy's disappearance, my auntie had started to appear more regularly in the restaurant. She didn't stagger as much as she used to, and she sent me for 'pure water' less and less often, some days not at all. I could see the determination building in her eyes as she turned her back to the past more and more each day. But of course there were lapses; on some days she'd lock herself in her room, after stocking it with bottles of spirit, not coming out at all till the next day to resume her solitary combat with reality. I watched and prayed for her; there was little else I could do.

'What is this I am hearing about revolutions and riots, and your name connected with it? Boy, I thought you had more sense than that.'

I was seated in my usual position at the head of the aisle, close to the kitchen door. I could see them through the crack between door and frame. Auntie Rachael was leaning against the draining board; Joshua was in the centre of the small kitchen, half-facing her, his head inclined a bit. All around them were pots and pans, dirty dishes in the sink and yam peelings on the floor.

'Don't allow these fools to drag you into this. That Ojikutu, or Mao, or whatever he calls himself, has always been a self-important no-do-good, and it seems his university education has only made him worse. But you, I thought you had more sense than that.'

Her voice was accusatory, as if she had discovered that she had been sold fake jewellery.

'I understand what you mean, Madam Godwill. But it is too late to go back now . . . I assure you it'll be simple and peaceful. That's part of the reason I am joining them, to make sure it doesn't get violent.'

My auntie's voice was low and sad and full of memory when she said, 'It is never ever peaceful, Teacher Joshua. Never. Look around you, can't you see they are desperately looking for someone to shoot or lock up? Don't give them the chance.'

When they came out, she stood beside me by the door and watched him walk down the aisle, nodding greetings at the eaters, till he pushed aside the bead curtain and stepped out into the hot sun. She patted my head absently and sighed. 'They want to make a martyr of him by force.'

She sighed again, still staring down the aisle into the sunshine.

To become a martyr, one has to get killed first. Killed for a cause. In ancient times the cause had to be religious, like some of the saints. Now, one could be a political martyr, like Martin Luther King, Jr, like Ken Saro Wiwa. The death of martyrs has to be especially dire and painful: Joan of Arc was tied to the stake and burnt; Ken Saro Wiwa was hung by the neck till he died. Mao said that hanging is perhaps the most cruel way to kill a person, and symbolic, to serve as a lesson to others. First they tie your hands behind you, so that you won't hold the rope and pull yourself up when the pedestal is kicked out from beneath you; and they blindfold you, so that you won't see the hangman when he kicks the world from under you. You won't see his face and come back to haunt him. The knot in the hangman's noose usually rests behind the head, loose and waiting to take up the slack when the firm is removed from the victim's terra firma. Apart from blindfolding, the hood (usually black, symbolizing death) also covers the tongue, which lolls out fat and obscene, and the saliva that trickles down it, and the blood from the nostrils. When the bottom falls from the victim's universe he also loses control of his sphincter muscles — he pisses himself and defecates — all this before finally dying of asphyxia. But if he is heavy the neck breaks, reducing the length of his body-jerking agony.

'Maybe he doesn't really want to be a martyr,' I said, trying to hide the turbulence in my voice. She looked at me, her expression distant, and ruffled my hair and sighed again before returning to the kitchen.

7

Lomba was the first journalist I had ever met. He came into the restaurant early one day — we always opened by ten a.m., but food would only be ready around eleven a.m., sometimes not till eleven-thirty — recently, since Nancy's departure, things had been harder for my auntie to manage. He stood in the doorway, slim, of average height and inquisitive of gaze. I had never seen him on the street before.

'Food is not yet ready, sir. Come back in an hour,' I told him. I was seated by the kitchen door, glancing idly at a book. My auntie had gone to the market to buy rice.

The man sat close to the door; I thought he had not heard me and was about to repeat my comment when he said, 'I am not hungry, I was just passing . . . Do you have Coke, or Pepsi?'

Some people stopped just to while away time. Most of them had nothing better to do, nowhere to go. They'd stay for hours, exchanging banter with my auntie. But this man did not look like one of them; he was better dressed, he reminded me a bit of Teacher Joshua.

He looked at me with his inquisitive gaze when I put down the drink before him. He had been staring out into the street. He sighed and said, 'I used to live here, you know, just across the road, in that brown house.' He pointed at the tenement house across the road.

'I see,' I said politely. I waited for him to say more, but he said nothing, only went back to staring out into the street at the ugly brown house across the road. There was a faraway look in his eyes; it was as if he was trying to recapture the time when he used to live in that house, or maybe he was finding it hard to imagine that he had actually lived there once. I went back to my seat. I was a bit disappointed; I thought he wanted to talk.

'I was writing a book, a novel. Two years,' he went on, still staring out. He had not yet touched his Coke. 'It was like a dream, a hallucination. I thought I could cure all the world's ills through my stories.' He gave a small laugh and looked at me. I wondered why he was talking to me. I put an attentive frown on my face; my book was suspended before me.

'And have you finished the novel yet?' I ventured.

'I don't know,' he said quietly. 'Someone told me that even if I finished it no one would publish it. That is true. Here in this country our dreams are never realized; something always contrives to turn them into a nightmare.' Now he sounded bitter. 'But that should not stop us from dreaming, should it, boy?' he added with a small smile.

'No. Joshua said that dreams are part of reality, and that we often can't know what is realizable till we begin to dream,' I said. That got his attention. Now he looked at me with more interest, as if he was seeing me for the first time.

'Which Joshua?' he asked.

'My teacher, Mr Joshua Amusu.'

'So he is your teacher. Are you Madam Godwill's relative?'

'Yes, sir.'

'What a coincidence. I came to meet your teacher, but he has gone out. I know your auntie very well; I used to come here to eat; your auntie would sometimes feed me for free. I was very broke then, and she treated me like her own child.'

He went back to staring into the street. It was almost eleven o'clock now; soon my auntie would be back. I wanted to find out more about him, especially about his book. I switched on the ceiling fans; it was already getting hot.

'My teacher, Mr Joshua, is also writing a book,' I said.

He turned and looked at me. 'He was in my office last

week. I am a journalist, he wants me to cover the demonstration — tell me about it, what is it all about?'

I shrugged. 'I don't know much about it . . .'

He laughed at my hesitation. 'I see you are a smart kid.
But don't worry, I am not one of the antagonists. I will give you
a message for your teacher. Tell him I'll definitely be at the
Secretariat to cover the demonstration. Tell him I went to
the slave museum at Badagry yesterday, and that while I was
there I realized why it is important to agitate against injus-
tice, no matter the consequence. Do you think you can
remember all that?'

I nodded. 'I will.'

'Good.' He put his hand into his pocket and brought out
his card. He handed it to me. 'This is my card, to remind you
of the message.'

His name was Lomba, the paper was *The Dial*.

'I will give it to him when he returns.'

He stood up to go. He paused at the door, and, as if as an
afterthought, he turned and looked at me and said, 'One day
you should go to that museum in Badagry. You'd find it very
educative.'

'I will,' I said. I stood at the door and watched him walk
slowly down the street till he was out of sight.

8

The day of the demonstration began like any other, but it
ended in confusion and death.

The shops and stalls and petty businesses did not open as
usual that morning; very early the people came out of their

houses and sat on the front steps, looking into the street expectantly. A band of youths, with Mao at their head, made the rounds from door to door, urging the people to come out. They put huge signs at both ends of Egunje Road, declaring it closed.

'I won't stop you from going,' my auntie told me, 'but be careful. Run at the first sign of trouble, because I know there will be trouble. I can feel it in my bones.' She stood before the restaurant, staring at the crowd gathering in the centre of the road. The crowd was made up largely of youths: boys and girls, and the men that always gathered at Brother's shop. There were also a few women; they looked a bit hesitant, a bit uncertain. Most of them had put on their Sunday dresses for the occasion. By ten o'clock, everyone was impatient to start for the Local Government Secretariat, the venue for the demonstration. The Local Government Secretariat was just two streets away from us, less than five kilometres away. We set off, with Joshua and Mao and Brother leading. Cars pulled to the kerb as we passed, people stopped, some came out of their shops and houses to watch us. They cheered our high-spirited, placard-waving procession without really know-ing what was going on. A large body of street urchins joined our ranks, and by the time we reached the Secretariat our numbers had almost doubled. The Secretariat consisted of two blocks of three-storey buildings; it occupied a huge com-pound surrounded by a high, barbed-wire-topped wall. The security men stood undecided at the gates as we approached. A deep, uncovered gutter ran along the front of the wall, dis-appearing to the back. Our group broke into two, one on each side of the untarred road that led into the Secretariat.

Our arrival had attracted attention: secretaries and file-clutching, anaemic-looking clerks stood side by side with fat, briefcase-carrying contractors to peer down at us from the balcony of the second and third floors. As if finally making up their minds that our group posed a threat, the security men pulled the gates closed, standing firmly before them, eyeing us uneasily.

'Open the goddamn gate!' someone shouted beside me, and soon other voices joined in.

'Open up!'

'Open the fucking gate!'

Joshua quickly went forward and stood over the culvert, his back to the gate, facing the crowd. He raised his hands and there was silence. I could see the sweat on his forehead; his shirt was wet at the armpits.

'Keep calm. Please, keep calm. Now we are here, our next step is to read to the military Sole Administrator our list of requests, then we'll go home. I'll go in now and invite the Sole Administrator. I am sure he'll be only too happy to come out and listen to us. Remember, we are peace-loving Nigerians and our purpose here is peaceful.'

He turned and casually extended his hand to one of the guards; the man took it after a slight hesitation. He shook the hands of all three in turn, then he talked for a while with them. The first man, a heavily moustachioed elderly man who seemed to be their leader, nodded at the guard on his left and the gate was opened. The eyes on the balconies left the crowd and followed Joshua and the guard escorting him till they disappeared into the ground-floor entrance. We waited, our placards now at half-mast. After thirty minutes, the waiting became strained. Finally, someone voiced our collective fears.

'What if dem hold am inside?' It was Brother. He came out before the people, marching unevenly on his good and bad legs to the gate and back again. 'I no like this.' His eyes were as red as blood; his black shirt absorbed the heat like a rag soaking up water, making him sweat in torrents.

Mao came out and joined him. 'They can't,' he said. He looked calm and cocky. He glared at the two guards as he spoke. 'We'll break down this place to get him out if we have to.'

The tension was suddenly broken when a bus came to a loud stop at the side of the road facing the Secretariat, and the girls from the Mayfair Hotel came tumbling out. Hagar was at their head. They were like drops of soothing rain on the dry, brittle atmosphere. A loud cheer went up among us. The girls raised their placards and joined us; even the married women, who hated the girls like death, cheered and embraced them. There were about twenty of them, their faces caked in inches of make-up, their impossibly huge wigs tumbling massive waves of hair down their shoulders. All were in jeans and T-shirts and canvas shoes. Hagar's eyes quickly scanned the crowd — seeking Joshua, I was sure. She saw me and smiled.

Then the gate opened. For a moment, as he came out, I saw the defeated look on his face. His shoulders sagged — just for a brief moment — then he braced himself to meet the questioning eyes. He raised his hands to silence the calls of 'Where is he? Where is he?'

'We've been ordered to leave . . .' he began, then he saw

Hagar. A quick transformation came over him, and from then till the end of the day, everything he did was sure and decisive. There was almost a swagger to his steps as he turned and headed for a garbage drum beside the gate. With the help of two men, he pushed down the drum, pouring out its contents into the gutter. Brushing aside the protesting guards, they stood the drum right before the gate and the two men helped Joshua up on to it. The crowd kept quiet; everyone seemed to notice the sudden decisiveness in Joshua's every move.

Joshua straightened up on the upended drum, with Brother and Mao on the left and right sides of him, facing the crowd, backing the Secretariat building disdainfully. He brought out a crumpled piece of paper from his trouser pocket.

'People — brothers and sisters. The Sole Administrator said he wouldn't come out to see us because our coming here uninvited is illegal.' His voice was drowned out by shouts of 'No way!'

Mao raised two fists in the air, roaring 'No' louder than anyone. He looked like a soldier on his way to the front, in his camouflage combat jacket and trousers and boots. The Mayfair Hotel girls raised their placards high, shouting taunts.

'But we did not come here to demonstrate, we came here today to pay our respects to the Sole Administrator, and though he won't listen to us, we won't go until we've said what we came to say,' Joshua shouted. He turned and glared at the helplessly staring security men before the gates; then he faced the crowd once more and unfolded the paper in his hands. At first his speech came out jerky, almost inaudible. From where I stood I could see the sweat running freely down his face. He was nervous; but gradually his voice steadied, and the paper, clutched with both hands, stopped shaking.

Now, looking back, I ask myself, if he was scared, why did he do it? What was he trying to prove, and to whom? I looked at Hagar and saw that she was not cheering as loudly as the other girls. Her face, beneath the make-up and the wide smile, reflected the tense anxiety in Joshua's face.

'. . . We have a right to complain to him, even though we didn't vote him into office,' Joshua's firm voice rang out, soaring above our heads and over the high Secretariat walls to the faces peering down at us from the balconies. 'And in a sense, this address is an accusation of this entire regime. We, the honest, peace-loving and taxpaying citizens of Morgan Street, are tired of waiting for the government to come to us. That's why we came. We came to tell you, Sir, that our clinic is run-down and abandoned; we came to tell you that we don't have a single borehole on Morgan Street and we have to go to other streets to fetch water; our schools are overcrowded, and our children have to buy their own seats and tables because the ones there have not been replaced since the schools were built ten years ago!'

His voice became impassioned; the people too: they shouted their assent to each point read out. Brother hobbled round the drum, nodding vigorously; Mao punched the air with both fists as if an enemy floated there, invisible.

'We are here to protest against this neglect. Where is the subsidized drug programme promised us from the Special

Petroleum Trust Fund? We need it now, because our children and our wives are dying from diseases. We are dying from lack of hope. And that's why we are here today to protest. And this is the way we feel we ought to express our displeasure.' Here Joshua paused and looked at the expectant people. The placards were high, like a faction's colours in a battle.

'First, from today, we refuse to be known as Morgan Street.'

'Yes Oh!' Brother shouted in his deep voice. He was facing the three guards by the gate, flexing and unflexing his arms, as if waiting for a command to charge at them.

'We don't know who Morgan was — some colonial administrator, perhaps, a reminder of our hopeless, subjected state. No, that name is too grand for us. We are a poor, neglected people. If we were to choose a name for ourselves, we'd choose a plain and simple one, something that reflects our reality. We do not know who Morgan is or was, but we do know what poverty is. We live with it daily.' Joshua squeezed the paper and raised his fist high; amidst loud cheering from us, he finished his speech. 'This is our decision: that our street, presently known as Morgan Street, ceases from this moment to be known by that name. It shall, from this moment, be known as Poverty Street!' He said the last with a solemn air, like a public executioner reading to the condemned the charges against him before he is executed. He reached down and, in what must have been a pre-arranged move, took from a man below a placard and raised it. The people roared their approval of the bold words on it: POVERTY STREET. Even the secretaries and clerks up on the balcony started to clap, catching themselves when they remembered that they were supposed to be the antagonists. He jumped down and was immediately surrounded by Mao, Brother, and two men with tiny recorders in their hands; one of them was Lomba, the journalist. Joshua's face was flushed and running with sweat, but happy.

'Well, how was it?' I heard him ask.

'Superb!'

'Good, very good.'

The first sign of trouble I saw was when a police van with only one passenger inside cruised slowly past and turned off the road towards the back of the Secretariat. The passenger was watching us keenly. Mao saw it too and pointed at it and whispered to Brother. The people milled about aimlessly, staring up at the Secretariat building; some waved their placards at the staring workers, others stood in little groups, discussing. Children sat at their mothers' feet, their faces alive with curiosity. I was standing with two boys of my own age, Ade and Michael, under a mango tree in the centre of the gathering, not far from Joshua. Now Mao was whispering urgently to Joshua.

'They've no excuse. This is a peaceful gathering. And in any case, we are through,' Joshua replied. That was when the anti-riot police came. They must have been positioned behind the Secretariat building for some time, waiting for a sign. Someone, probably the Sole Administrator, must have sent for them a long time ago. At the appearance of the anti-riot police, with tear-gas guns and batons and helmets and bamboo shields, a wail went up among the women. But Joshua quickly climbed the drum and shouted, 'Stay where you are, everybody. Don't move — stand still. Don't run!'

There was really nowhere to run to. The police were in two groups, on the north and south of the gathering; with the high Secretariat wall on the west, the only, but risky, avenue for escape was the busy road on the east. The wailing diminished; the police halted. They were in single rows, their bamboo shields raised high before them — they were about fifty in all, twenty-five on each side. All eyes, including those of the police, were on Joshua as he jumped down from the drum and headed for the police column on the north, where an Inspector, fat and furiously moustached, stood in front, tapping his leg with his baton, looking undecided. The Inspector turned and whispered to his men, and just as Joshua reached him, he did a curious thing. He raised his right hand and brought it down sharply. And his men charged. I could imagine the surprise, the puzzlement on Joshua's face before a baton hit him on the head and he went down. They trampled over him, like stampeding cows, and rushed on to us.

'Eeao!' Michael exclaimed and bolted for the road. I started after him, but Ade grabbed my shirt and pointed up to the leafy darkness of the mango tree. In a single, adrenaline-charged leap I grabbed a branch and hauled myself up. I did not stop going till there was nowhere to go. I fixed myself in the crook between branch and branch, panting, looking for Ade. He was to my right, clinging with both hands to a branch. But before we could congratulate ourselves on our narrow escape, the tear gas reached us. I closed my eyes, I felt trapped. Now I realized how small animals feel in a bush fire. The air below us was filled with scared wails and shrieks; women screaming the names of their children. But the dominant sounds were of batons on flesh, and boots on flesh, and tear gas popping out of projectiles. Suddenly the wind altered direction, blowing the noxious fumes towards the Secretariat building, and I was able to open my eyes. My eyes and mouth ran with fluid, my sweaty skin was pepperish with dissolved tear gas. But I could see through the mango leaves. The people, scared witless, hemmed in on all sides, stupefied by the choking tear gas, ran out in all directions, like quails beaten out of their hiding places, coughing and falling. Agile youths attempted to scale the high Secretariat wall, but they were swatted down by police batons, like mosquitoes, to fall into the open gutter, shaking and writhing with pain and terror. Those that were able to reach the top had their grasping hands cut to laces by the barbed wire on top. Others, mainly women and children, attempted to run across the road, only to be knocked down by speeding vehicles. I closed my eyes. I discovered that I was whimpering like a lost child. I couldn't help it. Even now, many years later, the distinct sounds of the violence echo in my mind whenever I think about it. I can still hear the thud of blows, the oomph! of air escaping mouths and the shrill, terrified screams of the women.

Minutes or hours later, when I opened my eyes, I saw Joshua and Hagar making a mad dash towards the now-deserted road, hand in hand. I was cheered. If they could make it to the other side they were safe; there were so many alleys and doorways they could duck into. But just as they reached the road, Joshua turned and stared back at the still-ongoing struggle. I saw the indecision on his face. But Hagar was still running, and she was in the centre of the road before she discovered that she was alone; she slowed down, turned and stopped. She opened her mouth — that was how the car hit her, with Joshua's name on her lips. The dull, loud impact dislodged me from the top of the tree and I tumbled down, hitting branches and leaves, nearly concussing myself on the hard, jutting-out root at the base of the tree. Then I was up and running for the road, tripping over prone bodies, clumsily dodging rifle butts. I met Joshua on the other side; he had dragged Hagar to the sidewalk and was seated on the ground, her head in his lap. He looked up when I stood beside him, his eyes were wild, all the earlier assurance and recklessness replaced by fear.

'Oh, my God! Oh, my God!' he muttered over and over again. His hands left bloodstains on her face as he brushed the hair tenderly from her eyes. There was a huge bleeding gash beneath her right ear; her leg lay at a twisted, awkward angle beneath her. She was unconscious.

'See the blood,' he said, unsuccessfully trying to stem the spurting stream beneath her ear.

'We must go,' I said. A policeman was staring at us from across the road; soon he'd cross over. 'We have to get her to the hospital.'

'Yes.' Joshua stood up. He looked at the deserted road helplessly; the hit-and-run car was nowhere to be seen. 'We must get a taxi.'

'Wait.' I dashed into an alley-mouth and soon reappeared on another street. I flagged down a taxi and hopped in. I directed him back to where Joshua was once more kneeling beside Hagar. When the driver saw the blood, he shook his head. 'No. I no wan trouble O!'

I remembered the four thousand in my pocket and took it out. I thrust half of it into his hands and said, 'Please, it was an accident. She is dying.'

I opened the door for Joshua. He sat in the back, with Hagar's head in his lap. But just as we were about to pull away, a running figure came to a stop beside us, panting heavily, staring over his shoulders.

'Please, I must come with you . . . they are after me . . .'

It was Lomba. I opened my door and he tumbled in beside me. We pulled away.

'See what they did to her. Look,' Joshua said to the reporter, his hands cradling Hagar tenderly. The tears ran down his face. Lomba was silent for a moment, staring mutely at the closed eyes, the heaving chest, the blood. His stare was so intense it seemed as if he wanted to remember every wound, every bloodstain.

'I am sorry,' he whispered.

'Just look,' Joshua repeated.

Lomba did not go all the way with us. He got out after about two blocks. 'Thanks,' he said. 'You have my card, don't hesitate to call me if you need me.'

I watched his slim, lithe figure dart into an alley, merging instantly with the shadows, and in a minute he was gone. He did it so quickly, so adeptly; it was as if he had been rehearsing how to disappear magically for a long time.

The taxi took us right up to the doorsteps of the emergency room.

'No. Don't come down,' Joshua said to me as I began to open my door. 'I want you to go with the driver and bring something for me from home. Here's my key. It is a small bag.' When the driver began to protest, he said, 'Please, you'll be paid. This is an emergency. God will bless you.'

He appeared to be in full possession of himself now. He described where the bag was in his room, then he got out. He lifted the still-unconscious Hagar after him. He shut the door with his leg and disappeared into the emergency room.

'Let's go,' I said firmly to the grumbling driver.

HAGAR DID NOT recover consciousness. I knew she was dead when I came back and found Joshua seated alone on a bench outside the emergency room, his head bowed. When he lifted his face, his eyes were red and heavy with unshed tears. I sat down beside him silently. I felt tired and empty. Through tear-blurred eyes I watched the nurses in their clean, white uniforms pass and re-pass. A white ambulance with a big red cross on its side came to a stop before the emergency room; its bloody passenger was taken out on a stretcher and rushed inside. Far away to our right were the wards: relations of the sick and dying sat in silent groups beneath a row of nim trees in front of the wards. The sun beat down mercilessly. When Joshua spoke his voice was hoarse, almost inaudible.

'Yesterday we quarrelled. She didn't want me to lead the demonstration. She even agreed to go away with me if I stayed away. I guess she knew . . .' His voice failed and he lowered his head again.

I loved her too, I wanted to tell him. She was the most beautiful thing I had ever seen. I thought of her young and beautiful body now lying somewhere in this building, on a slab, cold and inert. The emotions inside me were wild and confused and I just couldn't seem to think clearly.

'But I had to do it. I know some of the people there today didn't even know what it was all about. They thought it was fun to march and carry placards and sing . . . but some really understood. And I couldn't let them down.'

He looked at his hands and his shirt, as if seeing the blood and grime for the first time. The side of his head was swollen where the baton had hit him. His neck and cheeks were all bruised and swollen where the boots had trampled on him. 'It's all so messy.' He turned to me and put his hand on my arm, and now there was a sad smile on his face. 'One day, you too will have to stand up for something. And it'll take you by surprise. I just hope yours won't be so messy as mine.'

9

The police came the next day in their jeep. They parked in Egunje Road and dispersed in pairs, going from house to house, searching, asking questions. They said a curfew had been declared on our street: nobody was to be seen outside before six a.m. or after six p.m. Muda the pharmacist, and two other shop-owners who had POVERTY STREET on their signboards, were taken away, to return four days later looking bruised and starved. They refused to say anything about their arrest. Muda sold his business and left with his family for the village a week after his release. Brother was also taken away, but he did not return with the others. Mao disappeared and nobody knew where he went to; some whispered that he had been taken away by the secret police, but nobody knew for certain. We heard that Lomba, the journalist, had been arrested on the day of the demonstration, right after Joshua and I had left him on our way to the hospital.

For the one week that the curfew lasted, Poverty Street became a ghost town — the shops remained closed, even the schools and the Women Centre did not open. But a lot of people had reasons for remaining indoors: almost every house had one or more persons nursing a wound or a fracture sustained at the demonstration. Two people, apart from Hagar, died: Michael, my friend, who was also knocked down by a car, and Eniola, a pregnant asthmatic who was asphyxiated by tear gas.

My auntie did not open her restaurant. When the policemen came and knocked on her door looking for food to buy, she looked at them as if surprised by the request, and replied cryptically, 'I thought you people didn't need food and water like the rest of us.' She shut the door in their faces. There was a triumphant smile on her face when she came to my room and called to me. 'Come and help me clean some things.'

I followed her to her room. Her step was light, as if she was floating. She threw open her door and window. We took out every single item in the room: bed, seats, boxes, tables, carpet, photographs. Then we swept and washed the bare floor and walls. She did not falter or show any sign of fatigue in the two days that it took us to finish. She sang as she worked; she told me jokes and laughed loudly along with me. Even her face looked animated and young. When the room dried, she sorted her things into two piles: those that were going back inside and those that weren't. On the unwanted heap were hundreds of empty whisky bottles; old, mildewed, black-and-white pictures; and shoes and trousers and shirts from an old portmanteau belonging to her late husband which had been under her bed all these years.

'So much time has passed,' she said as she handled the unwanted things. It was the first time she had sounded sad since we started the cleaning up. Then she sighed, and almost literally pushed aside the darkness from her face. 'Well, I am sure some poor beggar will find some use for them. I have no use for them any more.'

On the third day, we went to Yaba market and bought new curtains, new bed sheets, and a new carpet. We stood in the centre of her room and clapped and exclaimed at the transformation. The light-blue curtains were a distinct improvement on the former heavy black ones. The room looked brighter, airier.

Tired from all the activity and excitement, we slept most of the next day. At six o'clock in the evening, at the start of the curfew, she came and woke me up. There were two men standing behind her. I had never seen them before. They were in suits; there was a solemn but mildly threatening air about them. Like policemen; but they were not in uniform.

'Kela, wash your face and come. These gentlemen want a word with you,' Auntie Rachael said. I heard the warning note in her voice.

She was seated on the bed; the two men were side by side on the couch; the single seat facing the couch was empty. I sat in it. The light from the open window fell on my face. There was something missing from the room. Throughout the interview the absence kept niggling at my mind, distracting me. The men looked identical in all respects, like twins; even their cross-legged posture was identical.

'Kela, we hope you can help us with our investigation. It is very important,' the man on the left said. 'We are from State Intelligence.'

I didn't know what State Intelligence was, but I nodded. I tried to catch my auntie's eyes, to get some kind of direction from her, but she wouldn't meet my eyes. Suddenly I felt apprehensive. Maybe someone had died. Maybe . . .

'Joshua Amusu was your teacher, wasn't he?'

The question jolted me out of my wild speculations. I nodded. 'He was.'

'And we understand that you were very close to him. You used to go on outings together.'

'Yes.'

'You seem to be the last person to have seen him before he disappeared after the unfortunate riot of last week. You were together at the hospital.'

I told them everything. Joshua had told me that they would come. He had warned me not to lie; that they'd definitely find out if I did. And in any case, there was nothing to hide.

'I left him at the hospital. He said he was going to Warri,' I said. I felt my auntie's eyes on me. I had not told her this.

'Oh, what for?' the one on the left asked.

'To see Hagar's people and tell them about her death.'

'And from there? Won't you come back?' I had asked.

Joshua had shaken his head. 'What for? Without her, Poverty Street will never be the same again for me. I'll move on,' he had said.

'Where?' I had asked.

'I don't know. I'll move around a bit. I don't know.'

Maybe he didn't want to tell me where, so that I wouldn't have to lie to them. I saw the excitement in their eyes as they leaned forward.

'Where was he going from there?'

'America,' I replied without hesitation. I saw the surprise in my auntie's eyes. The two men looked at each other.

'America? Did he tell you that?'

'No, no. I am only guessing,' I said, shaking my head.

'Why?' I could feel the restraint behind the word. Now they were trying to humour this fanciful child.

'Because that is where people go to when they can't live in their own country. They go to seek asylum.'

'I see. How interesting.' They were still humouring me. The tension in the air had reduced.

'But Kela, don't you think America is a bit too far to go to? There is a whole ocean to cross before one reaches there.' They laughed.

I shook my head patiently. 'No. It is not an ocean, it's just a tiny river. All you have to do is to imagine it. Wait, I am coming,' I said and dashed to my room. I came back with my Pathfinder's Atlas and spread it open before them. They were amused and a little intrigued by my earnestness. I pointed. 'See, this is Africa, this is Nigeria, and here is Lagos.' I drew a line. 'Across is America. If we could magically shrink up the ocean and reduce it to a little river, then all we'd need to get to the American shore is a tiny bridge. A walking distance, really.'

They laughed and stood up to go.

'But think about it,' I said. 'All we need is a little imagination to discover that things are not as fixed or as impossible as we believe.' I was trying to show them what Joshua had shown me, but all they did was pat me on the head and say to my auntie, 'You have a young philosopher here, madam.' And they left.

As soon as they were gone, Auntie Rachael left the bed and came and sat on the arm of my seat; she put her arms round my neck, resting her chin on my head. I was not used to this. My father only patted you on the back if you did well; and I had learned to duck under my mother's arms whenever she opened them. But I let Auntie Rachael hold me for a while. Finally she pulled back. There were tears in her eyes.

'Kela, my son, you must be careful. Never ever show them you are brilliant. They'll kill you. Don't you know that lightning only strikes the tallest tree?' Her eyes left me and went to the wall. And now I saw it: what I had missed all along. The soldier's picture was not on the table close to her bed any more. It was up there on the wall with all the others.

'Poor Davou. He was like that, too. He never learned to keep his head low. He was always standing up for something, for someone. He was among the very first to volunteer when the war broke out. They killed him.' Her voice was low and whispery. Her print dress smelled of camphor. Her eyes were not red any more these days, and the tell-tale smell was totally gone from her breath.

'Go,' she said, standing up, 'and always remember, our land is a land of pygmies. We are like crabs in a basket; we pull down whoever dares to stand up for what is right. Always remember that.'

As I left her, I recalled Joshua's words at the hospital: that some day I too would have to stand up for something. But did that mean I'd be pulled down when I stood up? I toyed with the question for hours, but I was unable to solve it. I finally abandoned it, deciding that perhaps I was too young to answer it. 'Not all things must be understood immediately,' Joshua had told me. 'The important thing is to see and memorize all the faces and ideas and impressions, and one day they will begin to make sense to you.'

MY EXAM RESULT came out a week after the curfew had been lifted. I passed all eight papers. I had A1 in Literature. But that only made me sad. Auntie Rachael was happy and she bought me a camera — but I'd have been happier if Joshua had been there to see it. My father sent for me a week before Christmas. He wanted me home for Christmas. I went to the beach the day before I left. I had the foolish hope that I might see Joshua there. I stood with my feet in the warm water and stared intently into the thick mist — as if expecting it to part and reveal Joshua standing on some shore in America. After all, the world isn't as big and impossible as we have been taught to believe.

JAMES

The day Sarimam walks out on Lomba begins unre-
markably, like any other day. No birds of augury cross the
sky, shrieking, casting long significant shadows on the
ground; no earthquakes and tsunamis rock the seas — at
least none that he knows of. The only upheaval he is aware of
is in his mind, his heart. She has left him for someone else.
They have lived together for a year, but this morning she told
him that there was someone else — that there had always
been someone else — and left.

'It won't work,' she told him. She said that she was leaving
him because he was too good for her. A perverse, back-
handed compliment. He sat down alone in the room after

she had gone, at the edge of the bed, staring at the wall before him, trying to ignore the pain in the bleeding hollow where his heart used to be.

'I've loved and lost.' That was the line that flashed over and over in his mind, like a May Day signal. He had once seen a sticker on a wall with the words, 'Better to have loved and lost than never to have loved at all.' He had thought it wise and deep at the time — but now he was willing to bet that the composer of those words had never really loved, not as truly and deeply and sincerely as he loved Sarimam.

Sarimam. Even the echo of her name brings him pain. He tries to lighten his dark countenance as he enters the editorial room of *The Dial*. Today is Wednesday, the lull day after yesterday's production frenzy. By tomorrow, the weekly tide will start building up again, the waves growing stronger through the weekend, finally to break on Tuesday's rocky shores. *The Dial* is a weekly magazine of arts and society, and recently politics. Ordinarily, Lomba does not come to the office on Wednesdays; he goes to the library in the mornings, and the evenings he devotes to Sarimam. But this morning, the day has stretched before him like a tundrascape, long, white and huge, without variety. That is why he is here. Because he doesn't want to go and get drunk, or stay indoors and cry; at twenty-seven he is a bit too old for that. The editorial room is half empty: only three people are there, one flipping through back issues, his legs on the table; another watching the TV without much interest; the last yawning as she files her nails.

'Ah, here comes the great Nobel Prize hope! Ladies and gentlemen, I give you Lomba, the defender of the arts pages,' says Seun, throwing aside a back issue. Seun thinks he is a comedian. That is not his only problem. He is also obsessed with sports — he writes the sports pages — and is fat, clumsy and club-footed.

'Lomba, the editor wants you ASAP,' Adam of the society page says in a clipped, military tone, without turning away from the TV screen, on which two semi-nude girls are dancing suggestively, pursing their lips at the camera. Adam is a stiff, unwieldy character who delights in talking about his years at the military school in Zaria. He was thrown out of the army ten years ago when he went AWOL.

'You look down,' Nkoyo says, blowing nail filings from her dress. Lomba sits down; his desk is next to hers. 'A little problem at home?' Her voice is incurious, but that is a disguise: she really wants to know if he has quarrelled with Sarimam — she knows they live together. Nkoyo is an intern; young and pretty and interested in Lomba. But to him, she is too young at twenty-one.

'The editor wants me?' he asks, not looking at her, arranging papers on his table.

'Yes. He came here himself to ask for you about ten minutes ago.'

James Fiki's office is on the other side of the building, across the reception lounge and down a corridor, next to the chairman's office.

'Ah, Lomba, come in, come in. We've been waiting for you,' James says as Lomba enters. He is not alone. There is a young man in one of the seats, facing him. The young man is in the middle of a sentence, his hands raised before him in illustration of a point. He lowers his hands and stands up.

'Welcome, sir,' he says to Lomba, extending his hand and pulling out a seat for him. Lomba shakes the hand. He has never seen the man before, who looks to be about the same age as him. The young man resumes his seat. There is an old-fashioned decorousness to his gestures and carriage, a gravitas that Lomba finds uncommon.

'This is Mr Joshua Amusu, from Morgan Street. He came to see you specifically . . . well, he'll tell you why,' James says. Ordinarily, James is fond of long, complimentary introductions; Lomba wonders why he is willing to relent today. He turns to Joshua.

'Mr Lomba, you may not know me, but I know you. I was your neighbour when you lived on Morgan Street, about two years ago,' Joshua begins. Lomba nods. He doesn't recognize the face, but that is not remarkable; the two years he spent on Morgan Street are now a blur in his mind; they'd been harsh and brutal years, filled with hunger and near despair, until James saved him.

'I am afraid I don't recall your face.'

'It is all right. I came because of a feature article you wrote on Morgan Street two years ago — about our abject condition. It was a good piece, it gave a lot of us hope. I still have it. I came in the hope that you would want to write something like that again.'

Lomba smiles. 'You want me to write another article on your street? What good would that do you? Nothing happened after the first one.'

The young man turns to James as if for help, but James only smiles and nods encouragingly. 'Go ahead, Mr Joshua, tell him about the demonstration.'

'We are going to have a demonstration, a peaceful one, next week, at our Local Government Secretariat, and we want you to report on it.'

Joshua turns fully to face Lomba and for the first time Lomba notices how intense the young man is. He has the build and the eyes of a fanatic — deep, sunken eyes that seem to glow in their sockets as he speaks; he has a thin, wispy beard to which his hand strays as he makes a point; and he is thin, almost emaciated. But his intensity is restrained, almost unnoticeable.

'A demonstration . . .' Lomba says, talking to James. 'Isn't that a risky thing to do at this time?'

'It is something we have to do. All we want is to draw the government's attention to our plight,' Joshua says. How simple it all sounds, Lomba thinks; but the man doesn't look like a simpleton.

'What if trouble breaks out? It usually does. The military government doesn't take kindly to such things.'

'They've decided to do it, Lomba. Our part is to cover it. That is all,' James says, not looking at Lomba. He has swivelled his chair to face the window, through which he is now staring. Lomba wonders why he appears so interested in the demonstration, and why he wants him to cover it — ordinarily this is a job for the political-desk guys; Adam, particularly.

'I usually write on arts and literature,' Lomba says stubbornly, deliberately addressing himself to Joshua. He wants to hear what James will say; he wants to know if this is an order. But James says nothing, he continues to stare out of the window. Now Joshua seems to realize that there is a subtext to the discussion. He looks uncertainly from Lomba to

James. He says, 'Mr Lomba, we felt that because you once lived with us and knew our problems . . .'

'He will come,' James says, abruptly swivelling round. 'I'll convince him. He thinks politics is for barbarians.' The two laugh. It is an order.

Lomba waits till the young man leaves, then says, 'I am waiting, sir. Convince me.'

The laughter suddenly leaves James's face and he sighs. He shakes his head and stands up. He comes round and rests his arm on Lomba's shoulder. He says softly, 'Tell me, have you finished your novel yet?'

Lomba shakes his head, wondering at the shift of subject. He has been working on the novel for over three years now, but somehow a satisfactory denouement has eluded him.

'But let us assume you've finished it. Let us assume it is a good book, potentially great. Let us say you've found a publisher to publish it — we are talking theory now, because in reality you won't find a publisher for it, not in this country.'

Lomba stares woodenly ahead, at James's empty seat. James goes on relentlessly, whispering his words into Lomba's ear. 'You won't find a publisher in this country because it'd be economically unwise for any publisher to waste his scarce paper to publish a novel which nobody would buy, because the people are too poor, too illiterate, and too busy trying to stay out of the way of the police and the army to read. And of course you know why paper is scarce and expensive — because of the economic sanctions placed on our country. But forget all that. Say you found an indulgent publisher to publish your book, someone who believes in this great book as much as you do; and because you are sure your book is good, you'd want to enter it for a competition — and what is the most obvious competition for someone from a Commonwealth country? Of course, the Commonwealth Literary Prize. But you can't do that.'

'And why not?' Lomba asks. He stands up and moves to the window, away from James, so that they stare at each other, the table between them, like antagonists.

'Because Nigeria was thrown out of the Commonwealth of Nations early this morning. It was on the BBC.'

They return to their seats. Lomba avoids James's eyes as he passes him.

'You can't write with chains on your hands.' James's voice is soft now, apologetic. 'Sorry, I had to be brutal — but you needed it. We are all in this together. That young man: I saw the doubt and uncertainty and fear in his eyes; of course he knows that in our country there cannot be a peaceful demonstration, the troops will always come, there will be gunshots, and perhaps deaths. He knows that, I am sure, but he is still willing to do it. The time has come when a few bruises, even deaths, don't matter any more. That's why I think you should go. To encourage him and show him he is not alone.'

Suddenly Lomba feels ashamed, ashamed that he has shown himself to be insensitive, even morally wanting. He nods. 'I understand . . . I am sorry.' James is his mentor; the one person he'd choose if he were to choose a role model. He'd want one day to be able to say exactly what he means, to mean exactly what he says; to shed all that is excess, unnecessary, so that at first sight his beholder could say, 'This person is like this, and not like that.' James is about fifty.

'I have something to show you, it will make you understand better why nothing must be taken for granted,' James says, smiling. He picks his jacket from the hanger behind him and puts it on. He adjusts his tie. 'Come, we are going to Badagry.' He is a tall man, over six feet. Lomba feels dwarfed when he puts an arm around his shoulders and steers him to the door.

OUTSIDE, THE SUN hangs low in the sky, red and opaque, the way it looks at sunset — but this is only noon. The heat makes the road ahead shimmer and shift.

'It will rain today,' James says. He has not told Lomba what he is going to show him at Badagry. The road is deserted on both sides, they seem to be the only commuters. Where has everybody gone too? Lomba wonders. It is as if a heavy threat hangs over the city — threat of a plague, or war — and everyone has parked their cars and locked their shops and run home to die before their hearths. Even the car radio is filled with static; the announcer's voice waxes and wanes unintelligibly. They pass Mile Two, pass the State University, pass Okoko, and soon the sleepy village of Badagry looms before them.

'We are going to the slave museum.' James shows his hand at last. The museum is an old, narrow, single-storey building on the beach.

'It is over three hundred years old,' James says as they park before it. It is made of stone — originally brown, it has now turned green because of the lichen and fungi bred on it by the damp air from the sea. The wood that supports the roof has totally decayed and the roof now rests on the building's shoulders, propped up by beams from the floor of the upper room. They meet a band of three bored-looking students being shown around by the old, sleepy guide. They do not join them. James has obviously been here before; he leads Lomba to a wooden shelf behind a glass partition where there is an array of variously shaped irons. Some are obviously chains; others are thin and circular; yet others are like bracelets, but cruder and thicker, wrought with no regard for beauty. They are old and rusty and utilitarian — and even if one didn't know that they were tools of slavery, their cruel purpose would still be unmistakable.

'These are the gewgaws of slavery,' James says, pointing. 'That circular piece is the mouth-lock. And that bracelet is the leg-iron. The round one is for the neck, it was used to join one slave to another with that chain.'

They move on, passing the group of students. One of them, a fat, small-eyed youth, catches Lomba's eye and yawns. The damp air from the sea makes the atmosphere heavy, hot. On one wall is a wooden plaque with the words 'SLEEPING SECTION', and an arrow pointing to the floor. They stand and stare at the plaque silently; Lomba imagines the bodies on the floor in exhausted sleep, waiting to be taken away in the morning.

'The word "sleeping" is a misnomer. The slaves couldn't have slept a wink. Imagine them piled in hundreds in this narrow space, chained, tired, broken and wounded: behind them lay family, friends, gods, land; and before them was the vast sea with the coffin-like ship at anchor, waiting to take them to another place, dark and unknown, and slavery, or maybe death by water. This was really a "sleepless section".

No sleep was slept here, and if there was, it was in fits and jerks. Let's go.'

Outside, they stand by the car and stare at a faraway ship approaching the port. 'It was in the ships that the mouth-locks were used, so that they couldn't console each other and rally their spirits and thereby revolt. To further discourage communication, no two persons of the same language were kept together: Mandingo was chained to Yoruba, Wolof was chained to Ibo, Bini was chained to Hausa. You see, every oppressor knows that wherever one word is joined to another word to form a sentence, there'll be revolt. That is our work, the media: to refuse to be silenced, to encourage legitimate criticism wherever we find it. Do you now understand?'

Lomba laughs shakily. The locks and chains have shaken him more than he thought possible. James's lesson is direct and effective, like a blow to the stomach.

A WEEK AFTER the trip to Badagry, Lomba is in James's car; they are on their way to the office after a visit to the National Union of Journalists' office in Victoria Island. The sun is low in the sky, tickling its spherical belly on the tree-tops and tall buildings; but it illumines less and less, and the heat increases.

'It'll definitely rain,' James predicts, glancing up through the windscreen at the low sun.

A girl, tall and fair, waiting by the roadside, makes Lomba think of Sarimam. They have the same way of holding their heads, bent a little, expectant. He wonders where she is now; probably with her new lover.

'You'll find somebody else. You'll love again,' she told him at the door before she left. She sounded experienced about it, as if he was just one in a long line of somebody elses for her. If only he had been able to tell at the outset that he was just being used as a rest station, a brief stop for refuelling . . . The beep of James's mobile phone brings his mind back to the present.

'Yes? Adam . . . hello . . .' He has one hand on the wheel; the other holds the phone to his ear.

'What breaking news? Dele, Dele . . . who? Dead?!' His voice shoots up, and Lomba stares at him curiously.

'Wait, let me park . . .' He turns to Lomba. 'It is Adam, from the office. He says they just got a report that Dele Giwa has been killed by a bomb.' He turns the car off the road abruptly, veering a bit too far on to the grass verge before coming to a stop.

'Adam, go on. I am listening . . .'

When he finally puts the phone down, he turns to Lomba. 'I don't believe this.'

Dele Giwa is — was — the founding editor of *Newswatch Magazine*, and the loudest voice against continued military rule in the country. He was among James's few close friends. James is staring through the windscreen at the empty road ahead.

'A bomb,' Lomba says, wanting to hear more.

'A letter bomb. It exploded as he unsealed it. He died at the hospital. Bomb. What a way to go,' James says. His eyes are still blank, still staring ahead. Lomba wonders what he is thinking. Finally, James starts the car. 'I told Adam we'll meet him at the office. We'll go to the hospital together.' Then he adds quietly, 'I have a feeling this is going to be a very long day.'

They do not meet Adam at the office; he stops them a block away from the office, appearing suddenly before them — as if he has been there waiting for a long time — waving frantically.

'Adam!' they exclaim together as the car passes him. James stops and starts to reverse, but Adam is already beside the car and opening the back door and jumping in. He is breathing hard.

'Editor,' he gasps.

James turns round and stares at him. 'More bad news?' he asks. He sounds calm, almost thoughtful, like a Stoic contemplating his end.

'They are there. They said they've a warrant to arrest you, sir,' Adam pours out, like a mortally wounded, faithful messenger delivering his message with his last breath. But he does not fall down and die. He goes on: 'I think you should move from here, sir. They may come out any moment and maybe recognize . . .'

'Oh, don't be so chicken-hearted,' James snaps, exposing for a moment his chafed, frayed nerves. But he starts the car and reverses in the direction they've come, then makes a U-turn. They drive in the thickening gloom in silence. Adam keeps wiping his face with a dirty white handkerchief, and looking over his shoulder through the rear windscreen. He is sitting forward in his seat, behind Lomba, his forearm on the back of Lomba's seat. He still has more to say, 'Also, Editor, they said they've arrested the editors of the *Concord* and *The Sunday Magazine*. Today.'

'All today?'

'Today, sir. You were next in line, sir.'

'Now I've spoilt what would've been an excellent day's work for them,' James says, aiming for light-hearted sarcasm, but not quite succeeding.

Adam, who has not a drop of humour in his body, answers dutifully, 'Yes, sir.'

Lomba feels like snapping at him to shut up. 'What are we going to do now?' he asks James.

'Drive around. See the sights.'

'Also,' Adam goes on like a broken record, 'I left them burning the hard copies of our next edition, and all the copies of the last edition. I think they came because of the caption on our last cover . . .'

'They'd have come anyway, caption or no caption,' James interrupts him and comes to a stop at the kerb. Lomba looks out at a huge neon sign before a burger shop. They are on Allen Avenue. The neon is dark red, ox-blood, like the sun above it. A lot of the shops have their lights on because of the thickening gloom. People are standing by the roadside, staring fearfully at the low, dark sun — it looks like a balloon that is fast losing air.

'You go to the hospital. We can't go together. Go and see what you can get on the Dele Giwa bomb thing,' James says to Adam without looking over his shoulder. Lomba knows what he is thinking: Adam's comments on the caption of their last cover have pinched him hard. At their last editorial meeting they'd all said it was a bit too direct, too confrontational: 'ABACHA: THE STOLEN BILLIONS!' But James had overruled them, and it went to press. Now perhaps he is feeling guilty about it. Adam alights. 'I'll go right away, sir,' he says with a small salute, and moves to the road to wait for a taxi.

'He was beginning to sound like a doomsday prophet,' James says. 'Let's go back to the office.' At Lomba's questioning look, he laughs and says, 'I am too old to play heroes. We'll just drive past. After all, we don't have anything else to do. Or do you?'

'No, sir.'

THEY SEE THE fire from about two blocks away. The smoke rises thickly in a stiff, steady stream, like an obelisk — as if conveying the essence of a burnt offering to the heavens. *The Dial* has a whole building to itself; the building was once a house, a duplex, before it was bought and converted into an office. It is in a quiet, residential neighbourhood with trees and hedges by the roadside. Both floors of the duplex are on fire. As James parks on the opposite side of the road, Lomba opens his door and makes to rush across the road to the burning building, where a small crowd has gathered. But James holds him back. 'Don't bother. It is too late. And they could be in the crowd, waiting.'

'The office is gone!' Lomba shouts, unable to understand James's calm indifference. 'At least let us get the Fire Brigade. Something could be salvaged.'

'Lomba, this isn't an accident. This is arson. Deliberate, official arson. The Fire Brigade must have been informed by a neighbour by now. But try again if you want.' He hands Lomba his mobile phone. Lomba dials. James watches the burning building in silence. Lomba almost screams into the phone, 'There is a fire . . . No. 5 Balogun Road. You have . . . ? Well, it is not here! . . . Do so!'

'They told you that they've already sent a fire engine,' James says calmly before Lomba can speak. Lomba nods. 'They said maybe it got held up in the traffic,' he says and stares ahead at the deserted road. They stare in silence as the fire rages across the road. Helpless fury forces tears to Lomba's eyes and he brushes them away with the back of his hand. He stretches his open palm out of the window and watches the ash gather on it. He holds the ash before his face and says in a broken voice, 'These very ashes could be from my pages.'

'An anonymous caller warned me this morning that something like this might happen,' James says as they drive away.

'You had an anonymous call this morning?' Lomba asks, repeating James's words.

'I did. But I didn't take him seriously. Now I do. He also advised me to carry my passport about — in case I have to get out in a hurry.'

Passport. Exile. Asylum. The association flashes through Lomba's mind and he thinks, has it really come to that? This morning everything was fine, apart from the heartbreak — and now even the sun has grown dark and is threatening to fall out of the sky.

'I'll take his advice from now on. Let's go to my house.'

LOMBA HAS WORKED with James for two years, but still he doesn't know where James lives. James is the type of person who partitions his life into neatly labelled compartments, with 'Work' placed as far away as possible from 'Family'. Lomba doesn't know if James has a wife or not, or children. Well, he will soon find out. James lives in Yaba.

'I've lived in the same house for the past ten years,' he says; his voice sounds nostalgic. Lomba knows that James is not the type to make small talk, so this bit of information is a sort of lament, an unconscious valediction, even; James can feel his ordered, rooted life coming to an end, and in front lies nothing but chaos, even exile — as for the slaves remembered in the museum.

'Here we are,' James sighs and enters a turning; he begins to slow down but suddenly his leg shifts from the brake to the accelerator.

'Where?' Lomba queries, looking out of the window. James is looking in the rear-view mirror. He takes another turning, and another, then he stops in a parking space before a supermarket. He is sweating, but not from the heat of the low-flying sun; it is an inner heat, a personal heat.

'There is a car parked in front of my house with two men in it,' he says, forcing himself to sound casual. 'A black Peugeot 504.'

People go in and out of the supermarket, some singly, some arm in arm, pretending that all is fine. *'Murphy's Mini Mart'* reads the sign above the supermarket.

Lomba says to James, 'If you describe the house to me, I could go back and bring the passport for you.'

James looks at him as if to protest, but all he does is sigh and nod his head. 'You can take a taxi from here. I'll wait for thirty minutes. If you don't return I'll come. Tell my wife to give you my passport and some money, foreign exchange. Tell

WAITING FOR AN ANGEL 205

her to go to my sister in Ikoyi early tomorrow. I'll contact her
there. Explain things to her.'

In the taxi, Lomba discovers that his hands are shaking.
His shirt sticks to his back, wet and dripping with sweat. He
feels like a cardboard James Bond as he alights from the taxi
and heads for James's house. The two men are still in the
Peugeot; he forces himself to ignore them as he rings the
doorbell. There are flowerpots outside the house with roses
blooming in them; when he looks closer, he sees that the
petals have started to dry and curl at the edges. The curtain
parts and eyes peer at him behind the glass door. He lifts his
face and meets the eyes, he forces himself to smile. The curtain falls back and the door opens.

'Mrs James Fiki?' he asks, trying not to turn and look at the
parked car. He feels eyes boring into his back like drill
points. The woman nods; her eyes dart past him to the
parked car. She knows.

'I am Lomba. Your husband sent me,' he says, and is grati-
fied to see the relief flood her face.

'Come in, please,' she says, stepping back. She is a tall
woman, taller than Lomba, as tall as her husband, perhaps.
She is slim, but not pretty. Her gaze is steady and direct, her
posture is sure but unaffected: all in all, the kind of woman
one would expect James to marry. She is in a housedress, a
flower-patterned gown reaching to mid-calf.

'James sent you?' she begins as they sit, then, as if remem-
bering her manners, puts in hastily, 'I've heard your name
from James, Mr Lomba. And I read the arts pages. You are
welcome, what can I offer you?'

'Thanks, Mrs Fiki. I don't need anything. And I really can't stay long. I left James not far from here. We were coming here when we saw the car outside — have they been here long?'

'All day.'

'You've heard about the fire, of course?' he asks.

She hasn't. 'What fire?'

'At the office. James thinks it is arson.'

She is doing her best to remain calm; she smoothes a fold of cloth on her thigh. 'Was . . . was it bad?'

He nods. 'There's a warrant out for his arrest.'

She catches the bitterness in Lomba's voice. Her agitation shows as she gets up and goes to the window; she parts the curtain and peers out at the car.

'This morning Dele Giwa was killed. What is happening?'

There is a picture of the family on top of the TV: father, mother, and two children — a boy and a girl. Where are the children? Lomba wonders. Away at school, perhaps. For them, all will seem normal. They don't know that for their parents the universe is slowly breaking to pieces.

'What is he going to do now?' she asks, returning to her seat. How will she take it, that her husband is contemplating leaving the country, as an exile, a refugee?

Lomba answers, 'He needs his passport.'

She takes it better than he expects. A brief silence, that is all, then she nods. 'I understand. And money?'

'Yes. Foreign exchange.'

When she returns with the two items, he tells her, 'He said he'd contact you at his sister's house, in Ikoyi, early tomorrow.' The money is in pounds and dollars, a thick wad held by a rubber band.

'Tell him to take care . . . not to worry about us. Let him do whatever he has to do.'

'I'll tell him,' Lomba says, then he adds, 'I am sorry.'

'Thank you,' she says.

He stands up to go. He asks, 'Is there a back door?'

She leads him out into a tiny courtyard with more roses in flowerpots. She opens the back door and peeps out carefully before stepping aside. 'Just take the path and you'll come out on the next street.'

But it does not work out that easily. They are waiting for him when he appears on the next street — one of them, really. He is in the obligatory black coat and dark glasses; he appears suddenly beside Lomba as he stands by the road, anxiously waiting for a taxi.

'I knew you'd take the back road,' the man says, grinning smugly at Lomba, pleased that his deduction has turned out right.

Lomba turns a blank look on him. 'Good day. Are you talking to me?' he asks as pleasantly as he can. He searches out of the corner of his eye for an alley-mouth to dart into, or a doorway, but they are right by the road, alone. No cars or pedestrians pass; only the huge, dark, evil sun hangs above their heads, looking down derisively. Lomba attempts to turn and walk away casually.

'Don't!' the man hisses. He nods towards his right hand, which is in his coat pocket and is customarily clasped around a pistol.

'What do you want?' Lomba blurts out, throwing away all pretence.

'Let's go to the car,' the man hisses again. Lomba notices

that the hiss is not voluntary, not part of the cloak-and-dagger accoutrements, but because the man's mouth is twisted: a broken left jaw that has mended badly. There is a scar on the jaw; it has been carefully concealed, but imperfectly, with a beard.

'What car?' Lomba asks, his mind like a trapped bird, flapping about, seeking a way out.

The man comes closer, shaking the hand inside the coat. 'Don't waste time. You must take us to him. We saw you pass together. Come on. Oya, let's go.'

'Don't you want to see what I came to pick up, the money, the passport?' Lomba asks, dipping his hand into his pocket.

'What . . .' the man begins, sensing danger, but Lomba quickly brings out his hand, clutching the passport and the foreign currency. The items act like a magnet: the agent's hand automatically comes out of his pocket and stretches out to take them. His eyes behind his glasses are also on the items, but Lomba's eyes are fixed on his face. When the agent's hands are on the items, Lomba springs into action: releasing the money and passport, he steps forward and pushes the man's chest violently with both hands. The man lands on the ground, on his back, shouting out a surprised oath. But the passport and the money are still tightly clutched in his fist — he is stunned by his fall, by the attack, but soon his hand will return to his pocket . . . Lomba turns and dashes across the road. A car screeches to a stop inches from him. He does not pause till he is standing at the head of a turning that disappears behind a house. He glances across the road. The man is up, the gun is out and pointing at Lomba. A loud bang, like a car backfiring, splits the air.

Lomba sees the man's hand jerk; something whizzes past his ear. He ducks instinctively, and runs into the turning.

JAMES SEES THE bad news on Lomba's face. He is in the car, looking at his watch, turning the radio on and off when Lomba appears and opens the passenger door.

'Is she OK?' James asks, not looking at Lomba, his body braced for the worst.

'Yes. But I lost the passport and money,' Lomba blurts out without preamble. 'They shot at me with a gun.' His body is still shaking.

James reaches out and takes his hand. 'Take it easy. What happened?'

Lomba tells him, his voice gradually steadying. 'I am sorry. I bungled,' he concludes miserably.

'Oh, it is all right. The important thing is that you got away. I can get ten passports today if I want to. I've friends. In fact, let's go and see one now,' James consoles him, and starts the car. 'He lives in Ikeja.'

But Lomba can tell that he is distressed. James says nothing as they drive — but his very concentration on the road before him is indicative of his attempt to suppress the turmoil in his mind. He will be thinking of his wife and children and how the seizure of his passport will affect them. Suddenly, the car begins to jerk and stall. James decelerates and they crawl on. 'We are out of fuel.' The finger on the fuel gauge flickers past zero. James lets the car roll to the side of the road. Finally, it stops.

'Well, well,' he mutters. This is about the worst thing that can happen to a motorist in a Lagos street. To run out of fuel. Ahead of them is a Texaco filling station, but like all the other filling stations it has no fuel. A long, undulating line of cars starts from inside the station and overflows into the street. Drivers sit on their car bonnets, wiping the sweat from their brows, waiting. Some of them have been there for days.

The sky rumbles, a light, half-hearted wind shuffles the dust by the roadside, and it begins to rain. The two look at each other with incredulity written on their faces; as if such a blessing is totally undeserved by them, totally unexpected. Forgetting their marooned, hopeless situation, they begin to laugh and exclaim like children. 'I said it, didn't I? I said it'd rain today. Didn't I, didn't I?' James shouts, slamming his palm on the wheel. Lomba pokes his open palm outside, catching the rain. 'You did, you did!'

At the Texaco filling station, the drivers abandon their bonnet perches for their cars' interiors, rolling up the windows, setting the wipers in motion; others lock their cars and dash for the service shop at the back of the station.

'So, what are we going to do now?' Lomba asks. They roll up their car windows; their euphoria has diminished. The rain is heavy, falling in fist-size drops.

'This is going to be a heavy one. Let's dash for that bar,' James says, pointing to the verandahed doorway of a bar on their side of the road. 'Ready?'

They scramble out, pelted by the rain on the short dash to the bar.

Inside, the bar is filled with people sheltering from the rain. The room is small, like someone's parlour; iron tables and chairs cover the little space — all the tables are taken.

'Psst!' someone whistles at them. They turn. It is a lady, alone at a table. She beckons them over. 'Come sit down.' There are two empty chairs at her table. They sit down. James removes his tie and carefully folds it before putting it into his jacket pocket. The bar is against the far wall, across the room from their table, which is near the door.

'You wan buy something? Make I buy am for you,' the lady, a girl really, offers when she sees James looking towards the bar, trying to catch the barman's eye.

'Thanks,' James says, bringing out his wallet. 'What will you have?' he asks Lomba.

'Coke.'

'I'd advise something stronger than that. I am not a drinking man myself, but I am going to have a beer. We need it. Get us two beers, and one for yourself.'

She takes the money and sashays her way past the tables to the bar. A group is standing at the counter, staring up at the tiny, black-and-white TV on the fridge behind the barman.

Presently, the girl returns with the three bottles of beer on a tray. She puts one in front of each of them and opens them.

'Thank you,' Lomba says.

She smiles sweetly at him. 'Na me go thank you, for the beer.' She is a sex worker, and extravagantly dressed for the part. The top buttons of her tight, almost transparent blouse are open, exposing the top of her breasts. She is wearing no brassiere and her nipples are clearly visible through the dress. She smiles, and bends forward, cradling her bottle in both hands, rubbing it against her chest. She can't be more than twenty-one, and quite pretty in a vacuous, unmemorable way.

Lomba turns to James. 'This rain won't go soon.'

James looks at his watch. 'Three.' But outside it is almost dark. The black sun hovers over the rooftops, still searing hot despite the rain.

'The place we are going to is not far from here. When the rain abates we'll walk there.'

'Who are we seeing?'

'A friend of mine. He is a writer, a poet. Emeka Davies.'

Lomba nods. He knows the name, he has read the man's work, though he has never seen him. Not face to face. He has seen him on TV and in the papers, vituperating the military. He does not hide his membership of the underground pro-democracy group, NADECO (National Democratic Coalition). Most of the group's members are in jail, or in exile — Emeka has refused to run away. 'I Am Not Scared of Arrest' was the headline of the last interview he granted Dele Giwa's *Newswatch*. Lomba notices that the girl has dragged her chair next to his. She pulls at his arm and smiles. She introduces herself: 'You no tell me your name, my own na Gladys.'

'Hello Gladys. My name is Lomba,' he says, casting an embarrassed glance at James, who isn't looking at them — his head is bowed tiredly over his drink.

'Lomba, which kin' name be dat?' she asks, and without waiting for his answer adds, 'I like am sha. I like you.' Her eyes meet his boldly. He turns away.

Someone claps his hands at the counter, asking for silence. They look up. The barman is fiddling with the volume control of the TV. There is a surge of bodies towards the counter, towards the TV. A hush falls on the room as the announcer's words reach them: '. . . Alhaja Kudirat Abiola,

wife of the jailed business tycoon and politician, Chief Moshood Abiola, was shot dead today by unknown assassins on
the expressway . . .'

'My God!' James whispers. A loud murmur follows the
announcement. Everyone is talking at once. 'The bodies
keep piling up.'

The girl is pulling at Lomba's arm, impatiently now. 'I get
room behind. Make we go.'

'No,' he says.

She pouts. 'You no like me?'

He shakes his head. The news has left him confused. 'I
like you . . . but I am impotent,' he says at last. 'I don't have a
gun.'

THEY LEAVE. THE rain has slowed to a drizzle, but the sky
still rumbles, the clouds keep gathering, choking up the last
traces of light in the sky; far away on the horizon a building
burns in leaping flames, defying the rain's pacification.

'The arsonists are still busy,' James mutters, glancing at his
parked car, which is up to its bumpers in water. The roads
have all turned into rivers bearing logs, items of clothing, a
cooking pot, a dead dog. They roll up their trousers and wade
grimly through the flotsam to the car. James checks the doors
to confirm that they are locked. 'I'll send someone to get it
later. Let's go.'

Lomba follows James through dim alleys and flooded back
roads; their shoes are heavy with water and mud. Often he
stumbles — the beer he has drunk makes him feel light-
headed and dreamy. Finally, James stops before a house gate.

'Here we are,' he says. They roll down their trouser-legs and
stamp the mud off their shoes. There are cars parked by the
gate. 'He has visitors.'

James pushes open the gate and they find themselves
before a front door caged in burglarproof railings. James
presses the doorbell and they wait in silence. Emeka Davies
comes down himself to let them in. Lomba recognizes him
immediately: tall and huge and bearded and light-skinned.

'James!' he exclaims, his pleasure lighting up his face. He
unlocks the security bars and engulfs James in a bear hug. 'I
was told they had taken you away! Thank God! Thank God!'

'This is Lomba, he writes for our arts pages,' James introduces after the hug. Lomba finds himself wrapped in the
huge arms.

'I am a fan. I read your pages religiously.'

'Thank you,' Lomba says, gasping for breath.

'Come up and meet the boys. Every writer in Lagos is here
today. We are having a reading for two young poets who were
arrested yesterday. Akin and Ogaga. You've heard about them,
of course?'

He leads them upstairs, holding them by the hand. This
makes climbing the dark, narrow stairs awkward, and Lomba
stumbles, hitting his leg on a step.

'Watch out. Careful. Careful.'

The sound of music reaches them before they get to the
door. Afro-beat. Fela. The saxophone blare twines itself
around them and drags them forward. The room is full and
noisy and brightly lit; the windows and doors are all open.
Figures sit on seats around the cleared centre where couples
dance close together. Everyone seems to be holding a beer

and a cigarette. At the door, Emeka claps his hands dramatically and calls in a loud voice for attention. The dancers stop. Someone lowers the music; all eyes turn to the newcomers.

'Hello, hello! Ladies and gentlemen, brotherhood of the pen! I am happy to announce that we have here with us a man who a moment ago we all thought had been arrested; a man whose office was this morning torched by . . . well, we all know by whom.' Everyone laughs; he goes on: 'Mr James Fiki, editor of *The Dial*. And with him is Lomba, also of *The Dial*.'

Loud clapping. The seated figures totter to their feet, the dancers disengage — all make a beeline for James and Lomba. They shake hands and hug and utter congratulations. Lomba finds himself holding a beer. Someone drags him to one side. 'How did it happen, exactly?'

Lomba gulps his beer. He doesn't know how to start. There are over five faces circling him, waiting; he feels like an actor on his first night, petrified by the lights, scared he'll miss his cue.

'Were you in the building when the fire started?'

He turns to the voice, grateful for the cue. 'No. We came and met the fire.' They are still waiting. But what more is there to say? 'Everything was burnt to ashes.'

'The bastards!'

'I'll write that into my new poem.'

'I'll use it as the prologue to my new book. It is just the symbolism I've been searching for.'

Hands grasp his. Names are mentioned. 'Nice to meet you,' he repeats at each introduction. A kaleidoscope of faces: some he has met before, a lot he is seeing for the first time. He feels his head reeling, but he quaffs his beer determinedly. When he moves, he staggers and almost falls. Someone holds his hand. 'Steady.'

He is led to a seat . . . He flops down and searches the room for James. At last he sees him standing out on the balcony, deep in discussion with Emeka Davies. The music comes to an end. A young, waif-like figure in a baggy jacket stands alone on the floor, a piece of paper in his hands.

He speaks: 'The title of my poem is "Now Is Time". It is dedicated to Akin and Ogaga and Dele Giwa and all brothers and sisters in the struggle.' He proceeds to read in a surprisingly deep and sonorous voice:

'Chains break
When they get weary of chaining
And the chained, like the chick within
The egg, waiting, is visited by Liberty's sunlight

Now is the time
To cast off our irons,
Time to step off night's threshold,
Time to redouble effort, like rowers
Approaching shore

Time is
Quicksilver, always fleeting, its favours
Ungathered, and once gone none can recall it,
Delay it, or bend it:

Now is time
To stifle for ever

The crafty demons of this earth that
Daily clip our wings. Now our sun
Is rising, our gloom lifting. Now is
The time to cast off the iron that binds us.'

'Nice, isn't it?'

Lomba turns, realizing for the first time that a lady is seated beside him. Her face floats before him, filmy, smiling. She is smoking.

'Well, what do you think?' she asks again, still smiling.

'Gratuitous,' he mumbles.

'What?'

'Our gloom is not lifting. Our sun is setting. Look out the window, you'll see,' he says to her.

'Are you a poet?' she asks; she sounds suspicious.

'I think so.'

'I am a painter. I am going to illustrate his next collection. He has three already, you know.'

'Who?'

'Dunta, the man that just read. Surely you know him?'

He shakes his head.

'You don't read poetry. Everybody knows him. He has given readings all over the world, and he has been arrested twice. He just got out of jail.' She sounds indignant, almost hostile.

'I am sure he is good.'

That mollifies her. She offers him a cigarette. He takes a drag, and feels the vomit rise to his throat. 'I am going to throw up,' he croaks.

Immediately, she looks alarmed. She holds his hand. 'Not here! Not here!' She pulls him up and leads him to the balcony and stands him before the railings. He bends forward and throws up. When he looks up, the sun is hanging right there before him, pulsating, dully glowing, like a huge spherical spaceship lost in orbit.

'Now our sun is falling, our gloom setting,' he mumbles, closing his eyes.

'Here,' she hands him her handkerchief. He wipes his mouth and thanks her. She looks older than forty. She blows smoke up at the sun and asks, 'Have you ever been arrested?'

He shakes his head. 'Almost. Today.'

'You really must try and get arrested — that's the quickest way to make it as a poet. You'll have no problem with visas after that, you might even get an international award.'

'I don't want to get arrested,' he mutters. She is standing right beside him now, her thigh pressing into his. In a corner, two figures are locked in an embrace. Someone rushes out and leans over the rail and throws up.

'Hi,' he says to Lomba, wiping his mouth with his hand, 'I am Helon Habila.' Another one follows almost immediately; he vomits and introduces himself, 'Hi, I am Toni Kan.'

They keep coming.

'Hi, Chiedu.'

'Hi, Otiono.'

'Hi, Maik.'

'Hi, Nwakanma.'

'Hi, Mike Jimoh.'

Inside, the dancers are back on the floor, in each other's arms, clutching the inevitable beer in one hand. There should be wailing instead of laughter, tears instead of beer, Lomba thinks desperately; this is a crazy, reversed wake where no one is allowed to cry, and which has imperceptibly degenerated into a bacchanalia. The woman turns suddenly and presses her lips hard upon his; her mouth is bitter, acrid. He pushes her away and staggers inside, searching for James. Someone grabs his arm. 'Come, let me introduce you to Odia Ofeimum.' He wrenches free and walks through an open doorway. James is there, still huddled in discussion with Emeka Davies. He looks up at Lomba.

'Lomba,' he says, 'I am not going.'

He looks old suddenly. Lomba has never seen him so grey, so wrinkled, so bowed, so tired.

'What do you mean? But we've decided,' he says. His head is clear now. He looks at Emeka Davies, who shrugs helplessly. 'Your editor is being silly.'

'You really must go.'

'That is what I had always planned, always believed I'd do when the time came . . . but now suddenly my courage fails me. I can't live in exile, in another country. I'd die.'

'You may die,' Emeka Davies says to him, 'but not in chains. Here, even if you don't die, you'll be in chains. James, stop being sentimental, we can get you out today, now. We'll cross the Seme border into Benin. Passport and money are no problem . . .'

James raises his hand resolutely, silencing Emeka. By the look on his face they know they cannot change his mind. 'What dignity would I have, over fifty in some cold, unfriendly capital in Europe, or America, washing dishes in a restaurant to make ends meet?'

Lomba feels obliged to try one more time. 'Why not sleep on it? You could discuss it tomorrow with your wife . . .'

At the mention of his wife he sees James's face tighten, but he shakes his head. 'What of you?' he says, facing Lomba. 'You know that after what happened at my house today, you are now on their list. You could take Emeka's offer in my place. Go to London, or America. You'd fare better than me, you are still young.'

'No. I don't think I am that important to them. I don't think they'll be looking for me,' Lomba says, a little confused.

Emeka laughs and claps him on the shoulder. 'They know you. They know everyone. They are paranoid. They know where you work, your hobbies, they know the name of your girlfriend . . .'

Lomba suddenly remembers Sarimam. But it is as if she belongs to another world, another life — even her face is getting blurred in his mind. Has that much time passed? As if to reclaim his pain, last week's heartbreak, as if to re-order his life, which is careering on an uncharted path, he says, 'My girlfriend left me.'

They look at him. James pats him on the back. Emeka smiles and says, 'Don't worry about her. You'll find someone new. You'll love again . . .' His final sentence is drowned out by the sound of his name being called loudly at the door. He stands up just as the caller rushes in.

'Emeka, come, they are here!' the man breathes rapidly.
'Who?'
'Soldiers! They are at the gate, asking to be let in.'

James looks at Lomba. He says, 'You must leave here now. I am sure there's a back door somewhere.'

They rush out after Emeka; they find him at the balcony, peering down. They see the green jeep parked right by the gate. There are about ten soldiers, each with a rifle. One of them is banging on the gate with the butt of his rifle. At that moment, a soldier looks up and sees them staring down at them.

Emeka turns back into the room. 'These idiots will break down the gate if I don't open it. Everyone must leave. Clean up the place.'

Lomba holds James's hand. 'Let's go.'

James shakes his head. 'No. I'll stay. I am tired. I am sure there's a secret room somewhere in this house. I'll take a nap there till the soldiers are gone,' he says with forced lightness. 'You really must go now.'

People are streaming towards the back door, some still clutching their drinks. Lomba pulls him into his arms and gives him a brief hug. 'Bye.'

They avoid looking into each other's face. Lomba flows with the flowing bodies. He finds himself beside the painter. 'Where've you been? I've been searching for you,' she says, flashing him a concerned smile, taking his arm possessively. 'Follow me, I know all the hidden turnings.'

He follows her. They emerge into a long, narrow alley that leads to another street. She leads him to a car parked by a restaurant. 'Hop in. This is my jalopy.'

He almost weeps with relief as he opens the car door and enters. He gives her a grateful smile and says, 'I don't even know your name.'

'Mahalia. My parents hoped I'd be a gospel artist — I ended up a painter,' she says with a grimace and starts the car. 'Maybe I'll try my hand at poetry; I could make it faster as a poet, get out of this fucking country.'

'Maybe,' Lomba agrees. His eyes keep scanning the buildings and street signs as they drive.

'Are you looking for something?'

He nods. 'An address. I have to cover a demonstration. The address is somewhere here, a Local Government Secretariat.'

'The Secretariat is at the next turning,' she says, then she adds, 'I was hoping you'd come along and get to know my place. After all, we might never meet again.' She stops in front of the Secretariat.

'I promised someone I'd come,' he says. He gets down. The demonstrators have already gathered before the building. Lomba recognizes the young man, Joshua, on a drum by the gates, giving an impassioned speech; behind him is the Secretariat wall, huge, topped with barbed wire. Suddenly a vision of handcuffs and stone walls flashes in his mind, like a presentiment; he shivers.

'Thanks,' he says to Mahalia.

'Maybe I'll see you again,' she says.

'Maybe.' He thinks of James in Emeka Davies' house and wonders what is happening to him at this moment, and if they'll meet again soon, or never at all.

'Maybe,' he repeats.

He watches her drive away, veering sharply to one side to avoid the dark, pendent sun before her windscreen. When she disappears, he turns and makes his way in the comfortless twilight to the gathering at the Secretariat.

AFTERWORD

I T WAS A terrible time to be alive, especially if you were young, talented and ambitious — and patriotic. A human-rights commentator once described the state of things in the Nigeria of the 1990s as:

> a roster of hundreds of political prisoners and others who have been detained arbitrarily by the military regime; the judiciary is in paralysis having [been] subjected to all manner of military interference, you have prisons in appalling states and public services in a [state] of collapse, every element of the rule of law has been thoroughly undermined and compromised by Abacha.

This was actually understating the matter.

Now imagine yourself, young, talented and ambitious, living in such a dystopia: half the world has slammed all sorts of sanctions on your country; you cannot listen to the radio without hearing your country vilified; you cannot read any international paper without seeing how much lower your country has sunk on the list of nations with poor human-rights records. The weight on the psyche could be enormous; all Nigerians became stigmatized by their rulers' misdeeds.

I think if there is a passage in this book that illustrates more than any other the lived experience of those years, it is the one where Lomba — journalist, aspiring writer and not much of a believer in political activism — gets a wake-up call from James, his editor. He is told that he can write his novel, but he might never get it published, or if he got it published he could definitely not enter it for the Commonwealth Literary Prize because Nigeria had that very morning been expelled from the Commonwealth of Nations.

Every day came with new limitations, new prisons. Perhaps some of these limitations would have been endurable if one could have found a moral basis on which to be loyal to the military rulers, if one could somehow have believed in the mission they were set on. (Like the Ghanaians had in the early years of Rawlins, or the Nigerians themselves had in 1984–5 under the regime of General Muhammadu Buhari and Brigadier Tunde Idiagbon.) But there was nothing to believe in: the only mission the military rulers had was systematically to loot the national treasury; their only morality was a vicious survivalist agenda in which any hint of disloyalty was ruthlessly crushed.

But the funny thing is that the military first entered Nigerian politics as messiahs, to save the people from the squandermania and blatant ethnic rivalries of the civilians (or so they claimed). The first putsch in Nigeria occurred on 15 January 1966. It was staged by a band of young military officers, led by Major Chukwuma Nzeogwu, against the civilian government that had come to power after the departure of the British colonialists six years earlier. The coup was one of the bloodiest in Nigerian history, with the Prime Minister, Sir Abubakar Tafawa Balewa, the Northern Premier, Sir Ahmadu Bello, and a lot of other prominent first republic politicians, mainly from the North, losing their lives. The coup failed and General Ironsi, the most senior army officer, became the new leader.

But Ironsi's choice was unfortunate; it only served to heighten ethnic tension instead of reducing it. Ironsi, like Nzeogwu, was Ibo, and a lot of Hausa officers, to whose ethnic group the late Prime Minister had belonged, saw this as an attempt by the Ibo to dominate the country by force. The Northern officers staged a counter coup, during which General Ironsi and many Southern officers were killed. It was this succession of events that culminated in the Nigeria-Biafra civil war of 1967–70.

The war, more than anything else, served to entrench the military in Nigerian political affairs — because of this, General Gowon's regime, which succeeded Ironsi and which executed the civil war, lasted a whole nine years. This was followed by the regime of General Murtala and General Obasanjo, which managed to return power to the civilians in 1980. From Ironsi to Obasanjo, the military had ruled for an unbroken period of fourteen years. The Second Republic that ensued lasted only four years, October 1980 to December 1984. But the Buhari-Idiagbon military government that ousted Shagari's Second Republic was in turn ousted by General Ibrahim Babangida (IBB) in a palace coup the following year.

Nigerians had by now become inured to martial music on the radio announcing another coup; the gun-toting soldiers on the streets had become a normal part of the landscape. Because we had never really known, appreciably, any other way of life, we came to accept our brutalization matter-of-factly. We were ruled by decrees and whims, human rights became not rights but privileges to be given or withheld by the new ruler in uniform. Fela, the late Afrobeat maestro, referred to this state of things when he said in one of his songs:

You can't dash me human rights
Human rights na my property.
You can't dash me my property.

(Incidentally, because of his bold anti-military messages, Fela was to serve multiple jail terms.) We lived with guns to our heads.

The de-professionalization and total politicization of the Nigerian military was to occur during the eight-year Babangida regime. The General was given the nickname 'Maradona' after the Argentinian soccer star because of his ability to dribble the country about. Bribery and corruption were turned into veritable tools of governance. Even the staunchly anti-military Wole Soyinka was somehow inveigled into accepting a government post under IBB. First, IBB promised to return the country to civil rule in 1990, but he pushed the date forward to 1993 using the Orkar coup of April 1990 as a pretext. But the General scored an own goal when, after the 1993 elections in which MKO Abiola, a Yoruba, ran against Bashir Tofa, a Hausa, and in which Abiola was generally assumed to be the winner, he annulled the election results. This historic event was to serve as the beginning of the end for the uneasy acceptance which the military had so far enjoyed. It threw the country into turmoil; the North-South ethnic polarization reached unprecedented heights. The South wanted blood. The country came to the verge of another civil war. IBB had to bow out in disgrace, putting in his place the unpopular Interim National Government of Ernest Shoenekan, which was to last only three months. IBB's exit was really nothing but a clearing of space for Abacha's entrance.

Although General Sani Abacha's rule lasted only five years, compared to Gowon's nine and IBB's eight, today when people refer to the military years in Nigeria, what they mean are the Abacha years. Whereas Babangida used bribery and corruption to rule, Abacha used plain, old-fashioned terror. There were more 'official' killings, arrests, and kidnappings in those five years than in all the other military years put together. Traditional rulers were deposed, newspapers were shut down and their publishers and editors arrested. Lomba is merely one of the less spectacular victims in a long pageant, whose ranks boast such names as MKO Abiola, former President Olusegun Obasanjo (present Nigerian President), and General Yar Adua (who, with Abiola, was to die in detention). But Abacha finally surpassed himself with the hanging of writer and political activist Ken Saro-Wiwa in 1995. Alongside this reign of terror, the looting of the treasury went on as briskly as ever before.

The *Economist* of 18 November 1995, commenting on Nigerian military rulers, had this to say about Abacha and his junta:

> The current gang, under General Sani Abacha, are the worst: repressive, visionless and so corrupt that the parasite of corruption has almost eaten the host. These days the main activity of the State is embezzlement. Unchecked it is likely to end in Nigeria's destruction.

It almost did.

It was a terrible time to be alive. Most intellectuals had only three options: exile, complicity, or dissent. Needless to say, there was more of the first two than the last. But with the killing of Saro-Wiwa, the world was scandalized. The sanctions mounted. The internal and external anti-military struggles became strident. The name of Abiola became a rallying cry for all lovers of liberty. Abacha had to go: nobody has a right to impose himself over others in this way. It is morally wrong.

But as with most plots that become too tight and unwieldy, a deus ex machina was needed to effect a suitable denouement. It was granted to Nigerians on 8 June 1998, when Abacha died of a heart attack.

What this story tries to do is to capture the mood of those

years, especially the Abacha years: the despair, the frenzy, the stubborn hope, but above all the airless prison-like atmosphere that characterized them. This I tried to achieve like most works of historical fiction are achieved: by making recognizable historical facts and incidents the fibres with which the larger fictional fabric is woven: Ken Saro-Wiwa, June 12, Dele Giwa, Kudirat Abiola, the riots, the student demonstrations, and of course the arrests.

But not all of the above events are represented with strict regard to time and place — I did not feel obliged to do that; that would be mere historicity. My concern was for the story, that above everything else.

Helon Habila
Lagos, January 2002